6/5/10

To GEORGIANNA

All Holi Blessings

To you!

rkellinas@yahoo.com

Falling in Love with
SOPHIA

Falling in Love with
SOPHIA

Robert Krantz

For Tricia, you are the story of my life,
so much love, so much laughter,
so many wonderful moments.
My heart is your heart, my dear.

And for Chris, Nicholas and George, you are the
greatest gift God has ever given me. Each of you is
a captivating, shimmering, and iridescent color
that has combined to form a beautiful rainbow
that God has allowed me to look upon. You have
made my life a pot-of-gold.

Introduction

In 1998, I was fortunate enough to act in, write and produce the movie *"Do You Wanna Dance?"* I know I'm biased, but I think it turned out to be a terrific little movie. Unfortunately we never had the money to promote it properly and were barely able to open it in a few theaters. It was an incredible feeling to be in the theaters and see the audience laugh, cry and be so moved as they watched the movie. So many people came up to me, called me or wrote me a note and told me how much the movie meant to them. Their kindness and appreciation left an indelible mark on me. It made me think for the first time that what I wrote might be meaningful to someone other than myself (and my mother).

One question they would always ask me was, "When are you going to make your next movie?" I wasn't sure, because just as I was trying to distribute the movie, my wife, Tricia, and I found out that she was pregnant. With triplets. On December 20, 1998, our sons Chris, Nicholas and George were born. From the moment they were born, they became the primary focus of my life. I've always thought that the greatest accomplishment I could have in my life would be to be a great husband and a great father. That is still my goal today.

During their infancy, something interesting happened. Every night, my wife and I would put the boys to sleep. We would take turns lying down with each of them, and as I would kiss them and say my final goodnight, one of the boys invariably would say, "Dad, can you stay a little longer? I'm afraid of the dark." I would tell them yes and would sit by the doorway, so that I didn't distract them as they tried to fall asleep. A couple of times, they would say in the darkness, "Dad, are you still there?" I would tell them that I was, and gradually they would fall into a peaceful sleep.

As I sat in the quiet of that doorway those many nights, I thought about marriage, family, and raising children. Eventually, I took out a yellow legal pad and turned on a small night light and night after night, as our three boys would slowly fall asleep I began writing what became "Falling in Love with Sophia". When I finished it, I wanted to make it our next movie. However, I wasn't able to raise the money to make it into a movie. One day, my wife suggested making it into a book that would hopefully become a movie. I thought that was a good idea.

What struck me many times as I was writing the book was that when remembering events from years ago, I would remember three or four critical points, but beyond that, I couldn't remember anything else about those particular events. It felt as though God had left just those three or four critical thoughts that I would need in my memory so that years later, I would have them for the specific purpose of writing this book. There seemed to be a purpose for my writing this book. But, would this book mean anything to anyone else? I didn't know. So, I gave it out to a group of family and friends. The response I received was significant, so I began to think that maybe this book would be meaningful to others.

As of my writing this, I have no idea whether this book will be read by few or by many. Will it become my company's next movie? I hope so, but I don't know. I simply felt as though this was the door that God led me to. For me, the publishing of the book is the opening of that door. What will happen when I open that door? That's where the journey begins. It should be an interesting one and I'm glad and grateful that you are on that journey with me.

Sincerely,
Robert Krantz
October 2009

Falling in Love with

SOPHIA

Chapter One

I waved a white napkin high above my head as I danced for my parents and relatives. The furniture of our small home in Chicago, Illinois had been pushed to the side, and everyone clapped as the music blared out from our record player. The year was 1968, and my parents were playing music they had just brought home from our summer trip to Greece. Our house was decorated in classic second generation Greek style: painted icons of the Virgin Mary, Jesus, and various Saints on the walls; oversized worry beads on the table; and plastic on the living room furniture that would only be taken off when 'special' company came over.

All of my aunts and uncles shouted, clapped, and sang out loud with my father, Harry Alexopoulos, and my mother, Georgia

Alexopoulos, as they watched me jump and whoop dramatically around the carpet. My Dad was just beginning his law practice and was always working long hours, so spending this much time with him was rare. My mom was working equally as hard as a stay-at-home mom watching over my sister Angie and me. No matter how tired my mom was, she always prepared a feast for all our relatives every Sunday. The moment you walked into our house, the smell of her cooking said, "This is home". The lamb, the butter on the spaghetti, the *horiatiki* (village) salad with olive oil, the potatoes cooking with the chicken, the honey on the baklava—a symphony of aromas for the senses.

Angie, who was a year older than me, waited her turn to dance, all the while yelling, "Michael, you are doing the dance the wrong way." I loved Angie, but she had a knack for driving me crazy. She had curly hair that she always tried to straighten, and she could get away with anything because she had a smile that made you love her. *Yia Yia* Penelope, my mom's mother, and our last living grandmother, sang along and didn't miss a word. The correct spelling and pronunciation of

Yia Yia is actually Yiayia (Yia-YIA), but everyone I knew pronounced it yEYE-yuh, with the accent on the first syllable.

Technically speaking a *yia yia* is a grandmother, but they are much more than that. In our families, they run the show. With a look, a heavy sigh, a barrage of Greek, a joyous laughter, a meal only they could make, or a loving hug, they are the keepers of the family. They make sure no one gets out of line, and that the family keeps headed in the right direction. I was only eight years old, but intuitively I knew why I was waving that napkin so joyously as I danced. Life was beautiful. We weren't rich, but we were happy. Before the Internet, I-pod, I-phones, Xboxes, blue-ray DVDs, CDs, high-definition TVs, and every other high tech gadget that has been invented to numb kids' brains, we had three simple things: Family, God, and a love for being Greek. What more was there to life? I knew at this young age that this was the life I wanted when I grew up. I was going to be just like my parents. I wanted to get married to a woman I could love forever and have children who I could love and celebrate our culture with. I also wanted to be close to God and do something worthy with my life. When I prayed, I knew He was listening. I just knew it. As I danced across the rug in our family room, it all seemed so simple. I had no idea how hard it would be to hold on to those three things: My culture, my family, and God.

What I learned at Church Camp – Lesson #1

"Something happened on that dusty road."

Culture, family and God all came together for me at one place in particular: our church camp. When I was twelve years old, my parents allowed me to go there for one week in the summer. It was the first time I was allowed to sleepover anywhere outside my own home. You see my parents didn't believe in sleepovers. Believe me, I tried. The conversation would go something like this:

"Mom, my friend Craig asked if I could sleep over …"

A chorus of no would come from Mom, Dad and *Yia Yia*, who would look shaken to the core that I even thought about this.

"Why?" I would ask.

"We don't know those people."

Those people were code words for *they're not Greek*. "I've been friends with Craig for eight years. What could go wrong?" I would ask.

"Listen Michael," my mom would say to me, "You'll turn your head and someone will slip something into your drink and then what? You're dead. And we have to bury our only son. You want to see your parents go through that?" Geez, never mind the fact that I would be dead, I thought.

I think somewhere in the early 1970s things actually started to loosen up a bit. That was until Patty Hearst got kidnapped. It didn't matter to my family that her kidnapping was at the hands of a radical group a thousand miles away from where we lived and had nothing to do with sleepovers. Not a chance. My family went on 'lock down'. For a decade. No sleepovers and any non-Greeks who got near us were viewed as a potential 'troublemaker' from then on. So, at some point I just stopped asking to go to any sleepovers.

But, fortunately, I finally had an opportunity: church camp. And it was a whole week long! Now, you may be wondering why my parents had a change of heart and let me go out and sleepover somewhere for a whole week. The answer was simple: everyone at the camp was Greek. Those were the magic words.

Seriously, I could have told my parents I was going to burglarize the neighborhood and go drag racing in the streets with a group of friends, and if I just finished it by saying, "Everyone there will be Greek," my parents would have said, "Okay. Just call us if you are running late."

Then they would add, "Let us know if you need extra money." This was the *only* time they would say that because God forbid the bill came and I embarrassed our family name in front of other Greeks by not having enough money to contribute my share to the bill.

On top of that, the camp was religious so our priest would be there, and there would be Greek girls there, which might mean a future Greek wedding. It was a slam dunk.

I really didn't know what to expect when I arrived that hot summer day. I got out of my parents' car, put my knapsack over my shoulder, and walked onto the campsite. My parents said hello to some friends, and

I started to walk over towards my cabin. As I walked through the camp, I paused for a moment to look around. I had never experienced something like this before outside of church. Everything was Greek: the kids, the language, the food. I had never seen this much "Greekness" in one place. It took me a moment to realize it, but I had officially walked into my Greek life. From that day on, my life was divided into two parts. I had my American life and my Greek life. When I went to school, I lived my American life. I played sports with Don, Scott, Brad, and Rob. We went to McDonald's afterwards and listened to Casey Kasem's top forty countdowns on the radio. And then on weekends or holidays, I lived my Greek life. I went to Sunday school with Stavroula, Niko, Gus, and Stathi and to GOYA (Greek Orthodox Youth Association) with Costa, Anthe, Demo, and Demetri. We ate Greek food and listened to nothing but Greek music.

On this first day at camp, I met dozens of kids that were just like me. They ate *macoronatha* (pasta with butter and cheese), *bakalava*, feta cheese, *tiropitas* (cheese pies), *galatabutiko* (custard dessert), and all the other Greek food we ate at home. They had *keftethes* (meatballs) sandwiches for their school lunch, too. They had *yia yias, papous* (grandfathers), *nounas* (godmothers), *nounos* (godfathers), *theos* (uncles) and *theas* (aunts). They disliked going to Greek school just as much as I did, too. They had been taken by the absolute beauty of being in an Orthodox church when all the lights were turned off at midnight at Easter, only to see the priest emerge moments later, from the dark, holding a single lit candle as we all sang triumphantly over and over again, Christos Anesti! (Christ has risen!). And all of us shared in the ultimate bonding experience: being asked by our yia yia, "Thelees na fas xilo?" ("Do you want to eat wood?) right before she whacked us with her *koutala* (her wooden cooking spoon).

As I walked around the sprawling ranch, and put my bags down in my wooden cabin, I couldn't wait to get to know everyone.

After our parents left, one of the first things we did was to get to know the counselors of the camp. I was matched up with a lady named Fay, who was in her thirties. She had curly hair and kind eyes that put you at ease when you were in her presence. If you spent a few minutes with Fay, you could tell she was a religious person. She was one of those people you just felt comfortable talking to. As we walked down a dusty dirt road toward the lunch hall, she asked me about what I liked to do and whether this was my first time at the camp. She then offhandedly asked me what I wanted to be when I grew up. I said, "A lawyer, like my dad. I want to help people. I think that's what God wants me to do." She started laughing. Not a mean laugh, but I think she thought it was funny that I thought I had it all figured out at such a young age. But then she saw that I wasn't laughing; I had meant what I said.

When she saw my face, she did something I'll never forget. She turned around and said, "Then, let's pray about it." Huh, I thought. Pray? Here? See, I'd basically seen my family pray in three places: kneeling at church (the consecration), before dinner (no holding hands, sorry), and maybe before bed (at least that's what we told the priest). I'm not saying that's right, but that's about all I'd seen. Yet, here we were with the bright noon sun over our heads in the middle of a dusty road about to pray. I thought, God forbid if some other campers walk by and see us praying. But, before I could say anything, Fay was praying out loud.

"God, you've heard what Michael wants to do with his life—to be a lawyer and to help other people. If this is your wish for him, I ask that you guide his life accordingly. In your Son's name, Jesus Christ, we pray. Amen."

She looked at me and smiled, saying, "C'mon, let's get some lunch," and that was it.

The way she acted after the prayer was as powerful as what she had said during the prayer. She went right on to the next thing as though she had utter and complete confidence that God had heard us and He was now in control.

As we walked towards the lunch hall, I had no idea that my conversation with Fay and the following week at camp would color my life in ways that to this day I'm still learning to grasp. I know this for sure: something definitely happened on that dusty road.

Lesson learned: God knows the dreams of your heart.

Chapter Two

God must have known the dreams of my heart, because when I started sixth grade, the cutest transfer student from Tennessee was assigned to our Spanish class at Pilgrim Park Junior High School. She was so smart that she'd skipped several grades and was a couple years younger than me. When she entered the room, I saw her from the side and even from that angle, I noticed her adorable smile. She said something to the teacher, and then she plopped down at the desk next to mine. She looked over at me and talked to me like she'd been my friend my whole life.

"Hi, Michael," she said.

How did she know my name I thought? Maybe my popularity in school had gone up, and I hadn't realized it.

"I peeked at the teacher's seating chart," she said as she scrunched up her shoulders and laughed quietly. She then stuck out her hand and smiled the most heart-melting smile and said, "I'm Sophia." I was in love. She had the most beautiful eyes. They peered out at you with mischief behind them. It was as though she continuously had an inner monolog going on inside her about something funny she just did or saw and couldn't wait to tell you. It just made you want to be around her.

I got to know Sophia in Spanish class over the next few weeks. When the class partnered up into groups, I always finagled my way to be with Sophia. I went from a "D" to an "A" in Spanish in no time flat.

One night, as my family was eating dinner, I thought I would share my new-found love with them. My dad was not home, so I wasn't sure if I should blurt it out yet. His law practice was growing, and he was working longer hours. We finally were able to afford a four-bedroom home with a pond in the backyard. By today's standards it wasn't big, but it felt huge to us. We had dinner every night at 6:30 PM. My sister and I had to be there. There were no excuses. *Yia Yia* was living with us and helped my Mom with the cooking.

As my sister Angie cleared up the dinner plates, I got the bowls of *rizogolo* (rice pudding) out of the refrigerator to put down on the table for dessert. I wasn't sure when my dad was coming home, so I cleared my throat and began.

"I met a girl at school," I stammered. No one even looked up. It was just a bunch of, "Great … Pass the wine … How was the rest of your day?" kind of responses.

"Her name is Sophia," I said with a bit more strength. Now, that got a reaction.

"Sophia?" *Yia Yia* said looking up hopefully as she tugged on her ever-present cross.

"Sophia?" said Mom, suddenly interested. In their eyes, Sophia had to be Greek. You see, Greeks believe that we actually own the name Sophia. If a non-Greek names their child Sophia it borders on blasphemy.

"What's her last name?" *Yia Yia* asked silently praying for the trifecta: Greek, same village, and a *preeka* (dowery).

"Graff," I whispered.

Somehow when I said Graff they heard the word "leper." Boy, talk about destroying the moment.

"Graff?!" blurted out my sister Angie with a laugh.

"Graff? What does that mean?" *Yia Yia* asked with a look of disdain and confusion.

"It means she's not Greek," Angie said to *Yia Yia*.

"Sophia. Its-uh-Greek name," said *Yia Yia*. Mom then turned to *Yia Yia* and started speaking Greek to her, making sure *Yia Yia* got the bad news in her native tongue. This was another sure sign that things were going south.

There were basically two times my parents spoke Greek. One, when we were shopping and a clerk was trying to sell us something. This is how I learned the words *poli achriv*o (too expensive) and *boufos* (idiot). The other time was when they discussed something at the dinner table and didn't want us to know what they were talking about.

Yia Yia absorbed the bad news and as everyone resumed eating she gave me a look and said something in Greek to me. Just then, my Dad came in and apologized for working too late. As my Mom got him his dinner, I asked her what *Yia Yia* said. Boy, do I wish I had just finished my *rizogolo* and gotten the heck out of there. Instead, my Mom explained to me what *Yia Yia* had said. "She's telling you that there is an old superstition," said my mom as she got Dad some food.

Oh, great, I thought, another superstition lecture was coming. We have a superstition or saying for every situation known to man: weddings, funerals, good times, bad times, in-between times. Whatever is happening, someone will throw out a superstition or saying.

"The older sister has to get married before the younger brother gets married," Mom said, translating for me.

"Or else?" I asked.

"Bad-uh-luck," said *Yia Yia* with a wink and an assuring nod. It's amazing, for someone who didn't like to speak English a lot, her English suddenly seemed to get a lot better when she wanted to make a point to you.

Gulp. Bad-uh-luck? I picked up my dishes and got out of there. For once, I was actually looking forward to doing my homework.

That weekend, there was a huge snow-storm. It was the kind that we always prayed for so that we didn't have to go to school the next day. As I watched the snowfall, I talked on the phone with Sophia.

"Have you done your Spanish home-work?" she asked.

"Not yet."

"Do you want me to quiz you?" I said yes. Anything just to stay on the phone a little longer with her, I thought. She then said something in Spanish and asked me to repeat it back in English. I struggled to get the words exactly right. "If you can make it ... through the snow ... to my house ... I will give you a ... *besso*." Man, was my mind rac-ing. What the heck was a *besso*? A cookie? A hug? A stick of gum? Why, oh why, had I not paid more attention in Spanish? Finally, I re-lented. "What does *besso* mean?"

"Look it up," she said and then hung the phone up.

I whipped open my school bag and grabbed my Spanish dictionary. My fingers zipped along the pages finally arriving at *besso*. I stared at the definition: kiss. I whispered to myself, "Oh, man, she'll give me a kiss." I had to get to her home. But, how in the world could I pull this off? Dad was out working. That was good. But, Mom was home, and she'd know if I left. I quickly concocted a plan that sounded brilliant to my youthful mind. I looked into the den where my mom was on the phone.

"Mom, I'm going to take a shower."

She looked up from the phone. "Come here," she said as she handed me the phone. "It's Despina Konaris."

Despina Konaris was the perfect Greek girl or G.A.P. (Greek American Princess) as we called her. Everyone I knew was certain that I was going to marry Despina someday. For Greek guys, there is kind of an unwritten rule: date all the "American" girls you want in your American life, but when you get ready to settle down, marry the Greek girl. In this case, it was Despina. Our families had known each other for years, we saw each other every

Sunday in church, and her dad was a lawyer, too. I spoke to Despina politely for a few moments and then handed the phone back to my Mom. I had more pressing issues on my mind.

I grabbed my winter clothes, bolted to the bathroom, locked the door, and turned the shower on. As the water ran, I put on my boots, winter jacket, scarf, and gloves. I opened the window and was about to make my great escape when I had yet another brilliant idea. Turn the water on hot. I thought the steam would *really* sell the idea that I was in there taking a shower. So, I cranked it up all the way and dove out the window into the snow.

I know, I know. What in God's name was I thinking?

Just then I heard the window from my sister's room slide open. It was my sister Angie, the ultimate nark. "Michael Alexopoulos, are you going to Sophia's house?" she yelled out. There's nothing quite like hearing your sister's voice blasting through a quiet winter night in your neighborhood to scare the living daylights out of you.

"None of your business, Angie. And if you say anything to Mom, you're dead," I yelled back. She slammed the window shut, and I began my trek. About ten yards outside of our driveway as I was knee deep in snow and now sweating up a storm, I began wondering if I was going to make it. As I stomped through the snow, my mind began to wonder. What if *besso* had two meanings?

And here's the little part I left out: Sophia's house was nowhere near our house. It was a mile away. But love is a powerful force and inch by inch, foot by foot, I made it to the street she lived on.

As I ran down the snow-lined street, I saw her family name on the mailbox. Christmas ornaments and decorations adorned their house. Through the living room window, I saw her dad and mom decorating a Christmas tree. Her dad was a strong looking man whom you could tell loved his wife. The way they kidded around as they decorated the tree was endearing. I started to wonder if I should just walk up and ring the doorbell. But something caught my eye. In a small park just next to their house, I saw Sophia under a light, carving something into a tree house as she waited for me. I paused for a moment and watched as she finished whatever she was carving. She then closed her eyes, tilted her head up, and made a prayerful wish. Just seeing that made it worth the trip.

As I approached, Sophia's eyes were still closed, and I could see what she carved into the tree house.

"Sophia and Michael ... forever"

She opened her eyes and saw me. She looked at me like God had answered her prayer. You don't forget moments like that in your life. "Wow. You made it," she said, making me feel like I was the most important person in the world.

"Yeah ... it ... was ... nothing," I said desperately trying not to show that I was about to keel over from the exhausting trip. I sat next to her and looked over at the carving. "I didn't know how to spell Alexa ... Alexo ..." she said as she struggled with my last name.

"It's Alexopoulos".

"Alex ... op ... oulos. Yeah. So, I just put our first names," she said with a smile.

"Don't worry. Everyone kind of messes it up. But, I'm really proud of that name." I then walked over to the carving and ran my hand over it.

"I guess that's forever," I said.

"As long as that tree house stands," she said with total sincerity. I turned and looked at her. As the moonlight gently lit her, I was only inches away from her face. Around us, I could feel the peacefulness of the settled snow, the stars in the sky, and the cool winter air. This had to be love. I even recall heavenly bells chiming. Then I came to my senses and realized those were hourly bells chiming.

"Oh, man. I've been gone an hour," I blurted out. All I could think of was the hot water still running in our bathroom at home.

Back at our house, my mother had just pried open the bathroom door. My sister Angie ran in behind her. "My wallpaper!" my Mom shrieked as she saw that all of her expensive wallpaper had peeled off the walls from the excessive steam.

Okay, so cranking the water temperature all the way to the hottest level wasn't a great idea.

"Oh, is he going to get it," said Angie with relish. My mom turned and smacked Angie with the paper.

"What are you hitting me for? Michael is the one who did it," said Angie.

That's kind of the way it worked in our family. Even if you weren't the guilty party, if you happened to be in the vicinity when Mom and Dad were angry, you got a *batsa* (smack).

As the snow continued to lightly fall, Sophia pulled out her cassette player.

"Do you like country music?" she asked me.

"I really haven't heard that much of it." She pushed some buttons on her player and I heard a ballad version of "Rocky Top, Tennessee". It was a great song. When it got to the part where they sang, "Rocky Top, you'll always be, home sweet home to me," Sophia smiled.

"This song reminds me of home," she said. She got up and came over to where I was standing and put out her hands. "C'mon, we can dance. I love to dance." I took her hands and as the snow that was blown by the wind from the trees gently fell over us, we danced to the music. As we swayed, I caught a glimpse of the word "forever" carved into the tree house. I'd never felt anything like this moment in my life. I remember thinking if life was full of moments like this, it was going to be great.

"Did you ever find out what *besso* means?" she asked innocently.

"Kiss," I whispered. Even at the tender age of twelve years old, I wasn't about to miss that cue. I gently leaned down and kissed Sophia. As our kiss ended, we stayed in each other's arms and looked at each other. A moment later, a bright light flashed upon us. No, it wasn't a message from upon high. Rather, it was a sign from the high beams of my mother's car, as she pulled up to the curb.

"Guess I've got to go," I muttered. Sophia quickly gave me one last hug. I walked to my mother's car and got into the dreaded back seat. As my mom began to drive away, I pressed my face against the window to catch one last glimpse of Sophia and the tree house carving behind her.

My mom drove down the road in silence. I kept waiting for the lecture, but it never came. My mother, God bless her, knew that I was in love, and she, in her kindness, didn't want to ruin what I'd just experienced. The next day, I heard her tell my Dad what had happened. I remember him calling it a puppy love and everyone laughed.

I think everyone knew I would end up with Despina. It was just a matter of time. Nobody ever thought that this thing with Sophia would become serious. I mean, that wasn't how my life was supposed to unfold. Falling in love with Sophia? But, there was something so special about her. It felt like she was the one I was destined to be with. I kept wondering what would have happened if she had transferred to a different school other than the one I went to. What if she had been placed in a different Spanish class? Would I have ever met her? Even at that young age, I wondered whether our lives simply happened by chance or whether there was an order to it.

What I learned at Church Camp – Lesson #2

"In Heaven there is order"

There was great order to what we did at camp that week. One of the exercises we were asked to do was to find out more about the Saint we'd been named after. In the Orthodox faith, the name we are given usually comes from the name of a Saint. So, each camper had to pin a small paper icon of our Saint on our collar and whenever we were speaking to anyone that day, it was supposed to serve two purposes; one, we'd be able to tell each other about the Saint we were named after, and two, to see whether we'd talk to each other differently now that we were wearing icons.

As far as I was concerned, this was a great opportunity to meet all the young female campers. There were so many of them that I'd never met before. So, that morning I was first in line getting my Archangel Michael icon pinned to my shirt.

I quickly came to realize that Mary was a very popular name. Nothing wrong with that name, but every time I struck up a conversation with a Mary and was drifting away from the religious questions into questions like, "Do you have a boyfriend?" or "Do your parents let you date?" I would see the Virgin Mary staring at me from a paper icon on her collar. Everywhere I went that day, I saw the Virgin Mary (sometimes even cradling the baby Jesus) giving me a look. By midday, I was actually saying things like, "How is Jesus?" as though this would win me some points. Finally, I found someone named Catherine. Eureka, I thought! But, within a minute, she told me that her saint had died by being placed on a wheel with steel spikes on it. I looked closer at her icon and sure enough, there were the spikes. I felt like I needed to pray at the end of each of these conversations.

I figured it was time I actually learned about the saint I was named after, the Archangel Michael. I headed back to my cabin and pulled out a book on Saints. As I tucked a pillow behind my head and began reading the book, on my bunk bed, I was fascinated.

The book actually described Heaven because that's where the Archangel Michael existed. I had never really thought much about Heaven. I always thought of God up there and knew that somehow he managed to help all of us out down here on Earth. But this book described Heaven in great detail. It said Heaven was a place of complete order and was organized into several orders of Angelic Choirs with beauty beyond compare. Surrounding God was a celestial hierarchy: the Seraphim, the Cherubim, Thrones, Dominions, Virtues, Powers, Principalities, Archangels, and last of all, Angels. Each of these entities served its purpose in God's kingdom.

However, one day, an angel named Lucifer revolted and said that he wanted to be as powerful as God. A war, unsurpassed by any before or after it on Heaven or Earth, broke out.

When this war broke out, God could have called on any of the most powerful orders that surrounded Him. Instead, He reached down to the lowest power in Heaven, an angel. He called on the Archangel Michael to lead the forces of Heaven against Lucifer. As the Archangel Michael fought Lucifer, he kept shouting, "Who is God?" to Lucifer. In other words, "You're not God!" This is what the literal translation of the name Michael means, "Who is God?"

Michael and the good angels defeated Lucifer and his bad angels and once again order was restored in Heaven.

As I closed the book, I sat back in my bunk bed and thought about what I'd just read. Up until this point in my life, I kind of just went to church and got along. I really didn't understand much of the Greek that was spoken there, so I relied on the sermon, the beauty of the service itself and of course *yia yia* theology (Orthodoxy with *Yia Yia*'s spin on it) to nourish my development.

What struck me about what the book said was that God had called on one of the least in His kingdom for the most important task. But, even more than that, I was taken by the absolute order that God had in His kingdom.

As I headed back out to join the other campers, I wondered if God had the same order in my life as He did in Heaven. Did God have a purpose and a plan for my life or was my life going to be a collage of unplanned events that hopefully would amount to something in the end?

Lesson Learned: God is a God of order and for each of our lives, He has a specific purpose.

Chapter Three

The year was now 2000 and much had changed, some of it good and some of it bad. I drove my car down those same snow-lined streets that I had run down as a kid so many years earlier. I pulled up to the house Sophia used to live in. I glanced at the mailbox and read the name of the family now living there. A mother played with her two children on the front yard. It's strange when you see someone else living in your memories.

I drove down a bit further to the park that Sophia and I had embraced in many, many years before. I was curious whether the tree house that Sophia had carved on was still there.

I parked the car, made my way over to a thick patch of shrubbery, and with some effort peeled it back. I removed some discarded wood. And there it was … the tree house we'd visited so many years ago. Dilapidated, tarnished, but it was still there. I wiped away mud on the wood as I tried to remember where exactly Sophia had made her carving. Just as I was starting to believe it was gone, I scraped away some dirt and saw it:

"Sophia and Michael ... forever"

I stared at it for a moment, remembering that beautiful winter night years ago. I turned back the hands of time, thinking about that night. Fortunately, Sophia was still in my life. We had been dating for the past year and a half. In between, life had knocked both of us around pretty good. I was glad we were both still standing. Just then, I heard a car door slam. I looked up and saw Sophia. She was laughing and smiling as she packed a snowball and threw it at me.

"You don't even have to remember what a *besso* is, and I'll still give you a kiss this time," she shouted. She ran up and jumped on me. "I've only got a half hour for lunch. Why did you want to meet here?"

I pulled back the shrubbery and showed her the carving.

"No way," she said as she gazed at the carving. "Look at that. We should cut it out and take it to my apartment." Sophia stared at it for another second and then realized I hadn't responded. She then turned to look at me and saw that I was down on one knee and had pulled out a ring box and opened it. Yes, it was that moment. Her eyes opened wide and her mouth fell wide open. Before she could let out a scream, and I knew she would scream, I chimed in.

"Sophia Elizabeth Graff, will you marry me?"

Then she yelled. "Shut up!" She did a 360 spin and stared at the ring again. "Shut up!"

"Is that a yes?" I asked.

"Duh!" She slid the ring on and then tackled me. As she lay on top of me, she spread out my arms and connected them with hers, moving them back and forth in the snow forming a snow angel.

"I'm so glad you came back in my life. You're my angel, Michael Alexopoulos and don't you forget it." We both laughed out loud. Fortunately, there was a little bit of a kid left in both of us.

As we pulled up to my parents' house, their annual family Christmas party was underway. Many of Sophia's relatives were in town, and my parents had invited them over. You could see just from looking in the front window that everyone was having a great time. As we walked up the driveway, Sophia's closest friend, Jerome Parker, saw us and came over to give us each a huge hug. Jerome was a forty-two year old African American who was simply amazing. He was nearly six foot four, thin, and had a slightly pockmarked face from childhood measles that hadn't been treated properly. But all you noticed was his infusive smile and infectious laugh.

As Jerome headed out to his car to get some Christmas packages, Sophia and I made our way through my parents' house filled with all of our family and friends. Sophia whispered to me. "So, nobody knows?"

"Just Todd. I wanted him to tape us announcing it."

Todd Klinger, who had been my best friend since law school, made his way over to me. Todd is the friend everyone wishes they had in their life. Whenever I was down, he made me laugh. Whenever I was laughing, he made me laugh harder. We had been through the trenches together in law school. After school, I went to work for my Dad, and Todd branched out on his own. Through a set of circumstances, we ended up starting our own law firm years later.

Todd held up the camera and surreptitiously conferred with me. "Battery's running low. Everyone here?" he asked quickly.

I looked around to see who was missing. My dad was still working, and I couldn't see where *Yia Yia* was. Just then, my sister Angie snuck up on us, like a silent assassin.

"Okay, what are you guys plotting?"

"Nothing" we all exclaimed.

"We're ... uh, looking for *Yia Yia*," I said.

"She's upstairs," said Angie. As I got out of there, Todd quickly switched subjects.

"Angie, you look great. Is Dimitri here?"

"We broke up," Angie responded.

"You're kidding. What happened?"

"Ask your law partner." I could feel the dreaded gaze of Angie landing upon me as she continued talking to Todd. What happened between her and Dimitri was a sore subject. As she turned away, I tried motioning to Todd to drop the subject.

"Hey, there are a lot of other guys out there," Todd said to her, not catching my signals.

As Angie grabbed a drink off a nearby tray, she looked Todd square in the eye. "You know, Todd, I'm sure there are, but I'll never meet them and you wanna know why?" Todd shrugged. Boy, was he sorry to God he ever got into this conversation.

"These!" Angie proclaimed. Angie held her wrists together as though they were bound by imaginary handcuffs. "You know what these are?" Todd winced. "Golden handcuffs," she said. "I've got a job that gives me money, it gives me jewelry, it gives me a car, it gives me everything I want, but it doesn't give me five minutes to find a guy that I can share it with. You know what women call that?" She dramatically held her hands up again.

"Golden Handcuffs! Not that I need a man to make my life complete. I don't. I'm just saying ..." Again, her hands went up in the air.

This time Todd finished the sentence, "Golden... handcuffs?" he said.

"Exactly," said Angie. With that, she finished her drink, put in on a nearby tray, and dramatically walked away.

Sophia and I made our way upstairs to *Yia Yia's* room. I peeked in to see *Yia Yia* as she finished praying in front of some icons. She was older and moved much slower, but she still had that same intensity about her.

"Hey, *Yia Yia*, are you coming downstairs?" I asked as she finished praying. As she got up, I noticed she had been kneeling on the unopened box of a brand new computer that I had gotten her. It had become her prayer stool.

"*Yia Yia*, I bought you that computer so you could use it, not pray on top of it." She looked at it and laughed at me.

"What am I going to do with a computer; I never learned how to drive a car?"

Sophia who was behind me laughed and it was only then *Yia Yia* realized Sophia was with me.

"Hi, *Yia Yia*," said Sophia.

"Hi," *Yia Yia* said, barely above a whisper. Well, you could never accuse *Yia Yia* of being a phony. If she didn't like you, you knew it. And she didn't like Sophia. Maybe it was because Sophia wasn't Greek. Maybe it was because Sophia was such a free and gregarious person. Okay, maybe it was the tattoo that Sophia had on the side of her ankle of a face sticking out its tongue like a little kid. Whatever it was, they never got a long.

Yia Yia said she was feeling a little tired but was going to try and make it downstairs. Sophia and I left the room and went down to my parents' room. Sophia took the wedding ring out of her purse and put it on her finger.

"You ready?" I asked her.

"What about your dad? Don't you want to at least call him? Maybe he's on his way."

"He'll just say he's working." She motioned to me to pick up the phone and call him. As I walked over to the phone, sadness came over me. So many times as a little kid, I had watched my Dad talk on that very phone while I played by his feet. He was so smart, so strong, never a moment of hesitation, always winning, always sure of himself.

When he would leave to go to work, I would get on that phone and pretend I was him. I would pull empty envelopes out of the waste paper basket and sort them out on the table making deal after deal. I was going to be just like him.

Unfortunately, those dreams I had of becoming like him never took flight. The years were not kind to our relationship. When I graduated law school, I went to work for my dad's law firm. For the next nine years, I was the golden boy. Every case I worked on was either settled in our favor or we won outright in court. Then we had a case against Blue Steel. It was over a copyright issue. Not my strong suit, but I felt like I could conquer anything at that point. Blue Steel had hired one of the best law firms in Chicago, O'Malley, Surhoff, and Kraft. It was a multimillion-dollar case that in the end I lost. It was a humiliating loss for my dad's law firm. The next day my dad called me into his office. I thought we were going to commiserate, but to my surprise, he fired me in front of all the employees. Our relationship was never the same. When I saw him at family gatherings or at church, we engaged in nothing more than perfunctory conversation. The damage had been done and there was no way to undo it.

So, as I reached for the phone, honestly I was hoping he was going to be working late and would miss our announcement. Why let him ruin another day of my life, I thought? However, my Dad picked up the phone on one ring when I called.

"Harry J. Alexopoulos," he said with panache.

When I heard my Dad answer with such flair, I knew right away he was in with clients.

"Dad, we're waiting on you," I said flatly.

"I'm still working," he said. That was his badge of honor; work. Still working. Always working. Never stop working. Work. Work.

Work. I looked at Sophia. What a waste of time this call was.

"Thought you might be on time tonight," I said.

"Probably not going to happen," he said.

"Well ... I've got some news," I said.

"Yeah?"

"I asked Sophia to marry me. We're going to announce it at the party tonight."

"Well, how about that. Congratulations. She's a lovely girl." I could hear him shuffling papers on the other end, continuing to work. What I was saying meant nothing to him. Finally, I put us out of our misery.

"Alright, well, we'll see you when you get home." As I hung up the phone, I thought how strange this was. As a kid, you think of the moment you announce to everyone you are getting married, and you imagine your parents hugging you. You don't think of your dad giving a muted response and telling you he's running late at the office.

I turned to Sophia, and we headed back downstairs to make our announcement. It was time to move on with my life.

Chapter Four

Father Jim Xanthos was fifty-five years old and was the new priest at St. Nicholas, the church my family attended. He was still getting to know everyone, but had an easy-going manner that made people naturally confide in him.

"I want you to know I've only been here a month, but I've already put on five pounds. So, I'm going to bless the food and then close my mouth," he said.

Everyone laughed and he then gave the blessing. Before anyone could dig in, I grabbed a glass and dinged it.

"On behalf of my mother, Georgia, my sister, Angie, and my dad, Harry, who will hopefully be here shortly, I want to thank Sophia's mother and all her family who flew up here from Tennessee for our party."

Sophia's mother, Cindy Graff, smiled and nodded at me. She was an elegant lady. I don't think I ever saw her with a hair out of place other than the time Sophia and I convinced her to join us on a rollercoaster ride. Of course we purchased a picture of her screaming on that ride, enlarged it, and put it on her refrigerator.

I knew this would be kind of a bittersweet moment for her and for Sophia. Mr. Graff had a heart attack and passed away when Sophia was young. Mrs. Graff had never remarried and eventually decided to move back to Tennessee. I knew both she and Sophia would be thinking about him after we made the announcement.

"Now, since this is the first time a lot of you are meeting my family, I thought you should know something about us Greeks. Outside of family, religion, and food, there are two things you'll always hear us talking about: one is our sayings, and the other is our superstitions. So, I thought you should know the difference between the two," I said.

I gave them an example, rattling off the best Greek I could muster.

"That means you should measure a piece of cloth eight times before you cut it once. This was our grandparent's way of telling us, 'You better really think about who you are going to marry, because you only do it once.'"

As everyone laughed, Todd leaned over and whispered. "Michael, the battery is dying. Twenty seconds left," he said.

"Now, an example of a superstition would be something like this," I said as I walked over and extended my hand to greet someone. As they shook my hand, I continued. "When two people are being introduced and their arms cross with two other people who are being introduced," I said, as another pair of friends shook hands and their arms crossed over mine and the other guests, "it means someone in the room is going to get married."

As we stood there with our arms crossing each other, everyone laughed. Just then, I noticed *Yia Yia* opening her door upstairs about to come down. She stood there for a beat listening.

"Well I have thought about it more than eight times and somebody must have crossed arms when they were introduced tonight, because ... Sophia and I are getting married."

There was a slight gasp from everyone, followed by a loud applause. Everyone quickly gathered around us: cousins, aunts, uncles, friends, everyone surrounded us. Finally, my mom broke through the group and hugged me.

"Oh, honey, I had no idea," she said. As she hugged Sophia, I glanced upstairs and saw *Yia Yia* Penelope retreat back into her room. Apparently, this was one party she didn't want to join. A moment later, Todd came up to me.

"I got it, but the battery is out. Do you have a charger?" Todd asked.

"Yeah, it's up in my parents' room, I'll get it," I said. Just as Sophia and I started to go upstairs, her friend Jerome ran up. In perfect Greek, he congratulated us. As a Greek school dropout, it killed me that he actually spoke better Greek than me! Jerome was the jack-of-all-trades and master of all. He could do everything and make it look so easy. You could bring up any subject or any new hobby and Jerome had done it, was doing it, or was about to do it. When he got out of college, he went to Greece, lived there for a couple years, and learned the language perfectly. Like I said, he could do anything.

After he hugged Sophia, I grabbed her hand and we headed upstairs to get the battery. As we got to the top of the stairs, Sophia yelled back to Jerome. "Hey, Jerome, remember, you're choreographing our first dance!" Sophia shouted.

"I'm already working on it!" he yelled back. As we ran into my parents' bedroom to get the charger, I just had to inquire.

"What does that mean exactly—he's going to choreograph the first dance?" I asked.

"I always told him when I got married, I wanted a special first dance." I think I looked as though I'd rather chew nails than do that, but Sophia gave me a smile that could melt any look off my face. I suddenly dipped her and gave her a kiss. As the noise filtered up the stairs, we had what would probably be our only quiet moment of the night together.

"Hmm, don't move," she said as she looked at me. She brushed her fingertips over my face as if she wanted to commit it to memory. "I want this to last forever," she whispered to me. She didn't say this as a fawning wife to be but rather from the hurt she had inside.

"It will," I replied, leaning in to give her another kiss.

"The battery," she said laughing.

"Oh, yeah, the battery," I said coming back to the real world. I walked over to my parents' closet and opened it. The left side was full of my mom's clothes but the right side was completely empty. No clothes. No luggage. Nothing. I stood there in silence for a moment.

"What's the matter?" Sophia said, breaking the silence.

"Where's all my dad's stuff?" I asked. I opened one of his drawers. Everything was gone. Another drawer, same thing. A moment later, my mom walked in. As I looked over to her, her eyes said everything to me.

Sophia left the room, allowing my mother and me to talk privately. Talk about bad timing. On the night Sophia and I announced our engagement, I found out my parents were thinking of splitting up after forty-three years of marriage.

"What happened?" I asked.

"We were arguing over who we would invite to the Christmas party," she said.

"That's it?"

"No. We've been … it's been rough, lately. I was going to talk to you after the party."

"Mom, you don't just leave someone after forty-three years of marriage over a party list."

"It wasn't just about the party list," she said with fatigue in her voice.

"What was it then?" I asked. I think I was looking for a sound bite answer and my mom knew the issues were more complex than that.

"You know Michael, my mother once told me, people argue about a lot of things during their marriage, but in the end, it really just boils down to five things they're fighting about: in-laws, religion, sex, money, and children. We weren't any different."

We got up and headed back to join the party. As upset as my Mom was, I knew my parents weren't going to get a divorce. In some weird way, I felt like this was just my dad making a grand stand to let everyone know he was angry about something so that all the attention would be on him.

Sophia and I said goodbye to the last few guests. A moment later, Fr. Jim came over to say goodnight.

"Call the office and we'll set up the counseling sessions. It will be a good chance for us to get to know each other, too," Fr. Jim said. The church had a new program that required couples to go through counseling sessions before they got married. I had heard a rumor that the reason the church started these sessions was that one couple had gotten into a fight on the way to their wedding reception and gotten divorced the next day.

"Do other engaged couples come to these sessions, Fr. Jim?" Sophia asked.

"No. I just meet with you together a few times and then individually," he said.

"Great. We'll call you next week and get started," I said.

As I closed the door, I looked at our family portrait hanging in the living room. It was one of those expensive portraits that took hours to shoot. I remember the photographer kept telling us not to smile, but to let the love come through our eyes. That just made all of us laugh even more. It took three hours before we stopped laughing and finally got that picture. What a great memory. But, as I walked by the portrait, I couldn't help but wonder where those happy people in the photograph had gone.

"How serious do you think this is?" Sophia asked.

"Just my dad being a jerk. A couple days, it'll blow over," I said.

Chapter Five

The next day, Todd and I were on the street corner outside of our law offices getting coffee from a mobile coffee cart. It was called Carlos' Cart and Carlos always had the music cranked up; morning, noon, or night, he had that salsa music wailing. It was great on the days when you needed a little energy to get going. As the morning street hustle and bustle whipped around us, Todd spoke over the music, trying to explain to me how worked up my sister had gotten the night before.

"Michael, I'm telling you, she's like this in my face," he said as he held his wrists together, "and she keeps saying, 'Golden handcuffs! Golden handcuffs!'"

"She's been like that since Dimitri broke up with her," I said.

"But, why is she blaming you for Dimitri and her breaking up?" he asked. We paid for our coffee and started heading to the crosswalk. The warmth of the fresh coffee took the bite out of the morning chill.

"Here's the deal. Angie and Dimitri were getting pretty serious, right? So, she finally decides to bring him over to the house. When he arrived, he came through the *front* door. Alright? Everyone has a great time. Everyone loved him. Now, when he was leaving, I inadvertently took him out the *back* door to get to his car."

"What's wrong with that?" Todd asked, trying to make sense of it. I explained to Todd that it was a Greek superstition. "Whatever door the guest comes in, he must go out the same door, especially if someone who isn't married is in the house. So, I goofed up and took him out the wrong door."

"They broke up?" said Todd.

"Oh, yeah, within a week. Now, to make matters worse, Angie's older than me, right? Since I was a kid, my *yia yia* has told me the younger son is never supposed to get married, until the older daughter is married."

"Another superstition?" Todd asked.

"Big one. Now, that I'm engaged to Sophia, it's like a double whammy. I've got to find her a nice Greek guy and get this monkey off my back."

Todd paused for a moment, looked away and then looked back at me, incredulous at it all.

"Here's the part I don't get," said Todd. "When I was a kid, I used to skip on the sidewalk, you know, 'step on a crack, break your mother's back' and all that. I'd go home and look at my mom, and her back was fine. So, by the time I was five, maybe six years old, I kind of figured out on my own that this superstition stuff was goofy, right?" He turned towards me, "So, what happened to you Greeks? You never figured it out?"

"I guess not," I said, laughing at our own nonsense. As we waited for the streetlight to change, I looked across and saw a blue Bentley pulling into the huge office towers of O'Malley, Surhoff, and Kraft, across the street. A beat later, Bernard Surhoff stepped out of the car, perfectly dressed and perfectly arrogant. He was the attorney that beat me in the Blue Steel case. A valet attendant greeted him as he stepped out of his car. As we stood there with our Styrofoam cups of coffee, we watched a thirty five year old African-American security guard open the door to the O'Malley, Surhoff, and Kraft law offices. A beat later, a young African-American child, wearing an oversized security hat hurried out, and helped the guard hold the door open.

"Bet you he doesn't even acknowledge the security guard," I said to Todd. Surhoff, true to form, whisked right by the guard, and entered the huge building, never noticing the guard or the little boy. Todd and I just stood there amazed at how Surhoff just pranced on by as though he was somehow entitled to everything.

We walked up to our dilapidated offices. It always took me a minute or two to get the key to turn just the right way to get our door to open. Finally, it worked. As we walked in, we saw Dena, our secretary and a forty-eight year old man with a friendly face named Stanley Nichols waiting for us. Stan handed

Todd his resume. "I forgot to leave this, yesterday," Stan said.

"Oh, thanks," said Todd. He introduced me to Stan and explained that Stan was one of the people he'd interviewed for a jury consultant position we were hiring for. A moment later, Stan headed out. As the door shut behind Stan, Todd tossed Stan's resume in the trash can.

"I take it, he didn't do to well," I said as I picked up Stan's resume from the trash.

"It was a so-so meeting. He's like a comedian."

"He was cracking jokes during his interview?"

"No, I mean he's like a comedian comedian. You know, he's got an act, tells jokes, and goes to nightclubs. His day job is jury consulting but at night he tries stand up comedy." I studied Stan's resume for a beat. Something seemed familiar about this guy.

"I know this guy. Stan … Stan the comedian. I think he's Greek," I said. I raced over to the window and cranked it open hurriedly and saw Stan making his way through the parking lot.

"Hey, Stan!" I yelled. He heard my yell and turned around.

"*Ellinas ese*?" I yelled, asking Stan if he was Greek. Sure enough, he answered me back in Greek! I don't know why but when a Greek discovers another Greek, it's like they just met their long lost relative. I had seen this happen throughout my life at parties, in airports, restaurants, in different places.

In Greek, I asked Stan what village he was from and he told me Sparta. So was mine, I told him! Suddenly, the wheels started turning. I couldn't resist. I asked him if he was married.

"No," he replied. This was my opening to set my sister up with a guy, and I wasn't going to miss it. I told him to come by next week, and we'd have some work for him. I closed the window and ducked back into the office. Todd stared at me.

"What did you say to him?" asked Todd.

"I gave him the job," I answered.

"What? Are you serious?" Todd asked.

"His family is from Sparta."

"Oh, come on, we're not just going to give this guy the job because his family is from some city in Greece."

"Are you kidding me? Spartans were great warriors," I said incredulously.

"Warrior? He's a comedian." Todd said in exasperation. Fortunately, Todd's phone started ringing. He rolled his eyes as he answered it. As I made my way to my office, I noticed a forty-five-year-old African-American man waiting patiently in my office. I turned back to Dena, our secretary.

"I didn't have an appointment this morning, did I?" I asked.

"That's Peter Witherspoon. "He said he was referred to you by another attorney. It's a child custody case," Dena said.

I made my way to my office and saw Mr. Witherspoon waiting patiently.

As I walked in, Mr. Witherspoon got up to greet me. My first impression of Mr. Witherspoon was that he was a likeable person but had been through some hard times. As he spoke about his custody case and how he arrived at our office, I could see that my initial observations weren't too far off.

He had been dating a girl for a few years. She got pregnant, and they had a son. They broke up about a year later, but Mr. Witherspoon kept making child custody payments and seeing his son regularly. But, then he lost his job as a city bus driver because of a back injury. Out of work, he began racking up debt and eventually had to file for bankruptcy. The judge reduced the amount he had to pay for his child custody payments, which he said made his ex-girlfriend furious and she began to make it very difficult for him to see his son. She switched phones, moved to different apartments and never left him forwarding information. He eventually filed a custody case in Texas and because she lived in Illinois, it was transferred to a courthouse in Chicago.

"And how did you hear about us?" I asked.

"I was down at the courthouse, trying to file a motion on my own. I wasn't having any luck. An attorney came over, and I told him about my case and he referred me to you. He said he'd contact you about a referral fee at some point."

A referral fee, I thought? Everybody wants a piece of the pie. Whatever happened to simply referring someone and not asking for something in return? I couldn't let these thoughts out, so I replied kindly. "That's fine," I said. "And how old is your son, now?

"Eight," he said.

"So, you have this son, out of wedlock, and for the last couple of years, you haven't been able to make child custody payments. I understand you went through bankruptcy, had credit card debt, and all that ... but on top of all that, you haven't kept track of any of your visitations. And your ex is now married, has a good job, has an income, and her boyfriend is presumably providing stability for your son ..."

Mr. Witherspoon nodded. It always sounds worse when the attorney repeats things back to the client. The client can't put their spin on things, and all they hear are the cold facts. I had to be straight with him.

"Mr. Witherspoon, we would lose this case if we went to court. My best advice is for you to try and work it out with her."

"I have tried," he said sensing I was about to end the conversation. "She's moving to Texas. I'll never see my boy again."

Mr. Witherspoon took a picture out and slid it over the top of my desk. "That's my son," he said. I glanced at the photo and didn't pick it up.

"Awhile back, I learned a lesson the hard way. This is a business. I don't let myself get caught up in that anymore," I said as I motioned to the picture on my desk and then politely slid it back to him. "Only two things matter. One is the law on your side, and two is having the money to prove it. And right now, your ex has got both of those things."

"Mr. Alexopoulos, I barely got this case transferred up from Texas. This is my last chance. I will take one afternoon a month with my son. I just want to see him. If I can't spend time with him ..." he said as his voice trailed off in quiet sadness. Seeing his desperation, a thought came to me. Maybe if I knew his wife's attorney, I could make it a one and done phone call and get him his one afternoon a month with his son.

"Who's representing your ex?" I asked.

"O'Malley, Surhoff, and Kraft," he replied. That's why lawyers never ask a question unless they already know the answer to it. We don't like surprises. O'Malley, Surhoff, and Kraft was not the name I wanted to hear him say.

"Do you know who they are, Mr. Witherspoon?" I leaned back and pulled up the shades in my office and pointed to the mammoth building across the way. There it stood, imposing, daunting, and threatening as ever.

"That building is O'Malley, Surhoff, and Kraft," I said. "There is no way they would take a small case like this."

"My ex is the secretary for the president of Crowning Oil," he replied. Well, that explained it. Crowning Oil was O'Malley, Surhoff, and Kraft's biggest client, and if the president's secretary had a jaywalking violation, they would handle it just to keep Crowning Oil happy. In some ways, I was relieved. This was a pro bono case for them, and I knew they were going to get it off their plate as soon as possible.

"Well, the good news is you are not going to go to trial. I know it's important to you, but they don't want to spend time on this. It will be a five minute conversation, and I'll tell you right now, they'll dictate the terms," I said. I got up to escort him out, handed him our new client packet, and went over our fees briefly with him.

As he went to shake my hand the picture of his son that he was holding slipped out and fell to the ground. I picked it up and glanced at the picture of his young boy in a baseball outfit. What an engaging kid, I thought. He looked so happy as he held the baseball bat posing for his picture. You got the sense that the turmoil of his parents' battles had not hit him yet.

"I'll stop by their offices and see if I can get a favor. But, that's it. One visit. I don't want you to have any illusions about this case going to trial." As he walked out the door, I felt confident I could get him the one day a month visitation, but I just dreaded going back to Surhoff's law firm. So, why bother taking the case? The truth was, it was a quick paycheck, and we needed the money. I wish I was more altruistic than that, but that was the truth.

Chapter Six

Sophia was sitting at the kitchen table at my mom's house, and all the *yia yias* were surrounding her like a hive of bees.

"Okay, I've got all your choices for the bands," *Yia Yia* said proudly. She read the list out loud to everyone.

"The Grecian Keys are seven hundred fifty dollars. The Grecian Sounds are seven hundred, and the Greek Gods are eight hundred." *Yia Yia* looked at Sophia. "Personally, I'd go with the Grecian Keys. I love them".

"Oh, that drummer," chimed in another *yia yia*. "He is so cute."

After a moment, they turned to Sophia for her decision. "I'm not sure I want a Greek band," said Sophia.

As you might imagine, the place went silent. I mean, rock bottom, hear a needle drop silent. You see, if the bride says she really doesn't want Greek food, the *yia yias* will be upset, but they'll let it slide. Choosing somewhere other than Greece for the honeymoon, not really appreciated, but they'll look the other way. Name your kid after someone other than *papou* or *yia yia*, that will cause a big time raucous, but it will blow over. But, saying you don't want to have Greek dancing at your wedding? That's a death wish.

"What you mean, you no want a Greek band?" asked *yia yia*, her Greek accent somehow seemed to get instantly thicker and meaner.

"All my relatives are coming from Tennessee. I was thinking we should have a bluegrass band play," said Sophia.

The *yia yias* just stared at Sophia in dismay. A blue what?

I was seated at a back booth of Giovani's restaurant just outside of Greektown in downtown Chicago, waiting for Sophia to show up and go over some of our wedding details. I saw the door open slowly and from the way Sophia walked into the room, I could tell she was upset. Then, it dawned on me that she had just been with the *yia yias*. Oh, brother, I thought. What could have possibly gone wrong? All they had to do was pick out a Greek band! How hard could that have been? Sophia sat down and brought me up to date on what happened. I tried to explain to her what the problem was.

All of these *yia yias* had been to many weddings through the years. At each one, they picked up a little something they really liked; this one has party favors that look like the Parthenon, that one has her crown with diamonds, another one has rose pedals tossed at her and the groom as they take their first steps together. As the years go by, the *yia yias* keep trying to create the *perfect* wedding. But like a run away snowball, they just keep adding stuff.

"Listen, we'll have as much bluegrass music at the wedding as you'd like, Sophia," I said trying to quell the storm.

"You know I wouldn't be crying about it," she said as she got teary, "But just talking about country music reminds me of my dad."

Now her tears made even more sense to me. She had told me this story before, but I knew it would make her feel better just talking about it again. She said that every night after dinner, her dad would go out on the porch and play the fiddle. After he died, she used to see his fiddle sitting in the corner of their family room and she never listened to bluegrass after that.

"But, lately … this is the happiest I've ever been, and I really miss that music. I feel like I'm ready to hear it again," she said.

I wiped away her tears as she continued.

"I guess, in a way, I feel like if that music is there, then … he'll be there." A waiter picked up some of our dishes and headed back towards the kitchen.

"Sophia, trust me, my *yia yia* had no idea that music meant so much to you," I said. "She and the other *yia yias* were just trying to help. They're trying to connect on some level with you, and I think they feel like you keep pushing them away."

"I know, I know. I want to get closer to your *yia yia* and her friends. But, since I lost my dad, sometimes it feels safer to keep people at a distance." Well, now we were even closer to the core of the problem. Ever since the death of her dad, Sophia let people in just so far and not an inch further. She felt that if she let someone get close, they would be taken away from her or something bad would happen to them. So, she felt it was best to keep them at a distance.

"You ever worry that you would do that to me? Keep me at a distance?"

Sometimes," she said. I looked across the table and smiled. "I'm not going anywhere, Sophia."

It would not be the last time I'd have to reassure her of that.

Chapter Seven

Going up the elevator to the law offices of O'Malley, Surhoff, and Kraft, my stomach dropped. It was embarrassing to be there and revisit the scene where my law career basically came to an end. But, I needed the money.

I walked up to the receptionist and told her I was there to see Surhoff. As I waited in the reception area, I looked at the headlines from their big trial wins that dotted the walls. I couldn't help but pause at the headline of the case I lost.

"SURHOFF MAKES ALEXOPOULOS FEEL BLUE IN STEEL STUNNER"

Painful. Simply, gut wrenchingly painful. It was like looking at a car crash that I'd been in. For some reason, I couldn't turn away from it. If only I could switch our names around. How different my life would be if it said, "ALEXOPOULOS MAKES SURHOFF FEEL BLUE IN STEEL STUNNER," I thought. But that is not how the hands of fate played out.

"Mr. Surhoff can see you now," said the receptionist. I walked up to a large meeting room that had glass walls and a stunning view of the lakefront. Man, were these guys living large. I saw Surhoff and a row of lawyers eating lunch and enjoying themselves. As I walked in, he greeted me as only Surhoff could.

"Mr. Alexis!" he said grandly.

"It's Alexopoulos," I said grinding out a fake smile. Every time this jerk was around me, he intentionally butchered my last name to get a rise out of me.

My *Papou* (grandfather) once told me that when you are dealing with Greeks, the only thing you should never mess with is their pride. He meant it, too. Once when my family took a trip to Disneyland, we went on the "It's a Small World" ride. On this ride, you sit in a small boat and as you travel along, you see the flags and costumes of many countries and cultures from around the world. Well, half way through the ride, my *Papou* started saying, "Where is thee Greece? I no see thee Greece." By the end of the ride, everyone in the boat was looking in every direction for anything or anyone that looked like it represented Greece. But, no such luck. To say that *Papou* was disgusted is putting it mildly. After the ride was over, I went and had my picture taken with Mickey Mouse. As Mickey's helpers were about to take my picture with Mickey, my *Papou* made his way over. He looked at Mickey and said, "You no like thee Greece?" Mickey extended his hands wide as though he was happy to see *Papou. Papou* made the same exaggerated gesture right back at Mickey and then repeated the question. My *Papou* didn't understand that Mickey is not allowed to speak. He basically has two gestures: happy and embarrassed. Mickey then put his hands over his nose, and tried the gesture showing he was embarrassed. That one didn't go over with *Papou,* either. "You tell thee Mr. Disney I would like to see him," said *Papou*, as he sat down and began waiting for Mr. Disney.

Finally, my parents got *Papou* and explained that Mr. Disney had died years ago and that it must have just been an awful oversight by Mr. Disney that they forgot the Greek flag. My *Papou* never spent another dollar at Disneyland and every time a Disney show came on after that, one of us would have to go change the TV station. So, pride is a big thing in our culture.

"Never did learn how to pronounce your name, did I? C'mon, all your countrymen have cut their names short. I just saved you some time," said Surhoff as his minions around him laughed. "So what can I do for you?" He knew what I was there for. He just wanted me to kiss his ring before proceeding.

"A man named Peter Witherspoon stopped by my—"

"Despicable man, isn't he?" Surhoff said, cutting me off.

"Well, I just met him. Anyway, he mentioned that you were representing the mother of his child, and I thought I'd stop by and see if we could work something out."

Surhoff got up and casually started doing upper body stretches as he spoke to me. The message was clear: you are not worthy of my time.

"Legally, he doesn't have a chance. Morally, the man is bankrupt," said Surhoff. He glanced around the room. "Who's familiar with the case?" A few attorneys' hands went up lazily, as they continued to eat. "Does one day every couple of months sound about right to you guys?" The lawyers wiped their mouths and nodded their approval. "Sold!" he said with a smile. "One day, every two months."

He knew this was outrageous to offer. One day, every two months? He just wanted to see if I would fight him. As I stared at this pompous group, I bit my tongue and kept thinking it was five minutes and a paycheck.

"Okay, let me run it by my client. He, uh, he seems like a reasonable man." I turned and began to leave the room.

"Mr. Alexis!" Surhoff shouted. I turned. It was just a natural instinct, but, yeah, I turned when he purposely messed up my name. "See, you turned. I think you rather like that name." As the other attorneys laughed, he continued. "The visits will be supervised." Surhoff did this for no other reason than to give me one last swift kick in my rear before I got out the door. I nodded and got out of there before I said something stupid. Bottom line was that Mr. Witherspoon would be happy he'd get to see his kid again. Yes, the terms were demeaning, but what could I do? They had the upper hand.

As I got on the elevator, I looked back through the glass partition and saw all the lawyers laughing and joking around. I found it amazing that a child's future was just decided and no one cared the slightest.

As the elevator doors closed, I punched the button for the first floor and the elevator began to descend. The lights overhead cast shadows. Off of the elevator circuit board, I could see the silhouette of my face staring back at me, somewhat unrecognizable. It seemed fitting. I was a shadow of the lawyer I dreamt of being; this meeting crystallized that for me. Did I take my best swings at this case? No. But, I had to be realistic. I really wasn't in the game anymore.

What I learned at Church Camp – Lesson #3

"Take your swings."

One day, the counselors were playing the campers in a softball game. This was not an ordinary softball game. The campers had never beaten the counselors, but early on we had taken the lead. History was in the making, I thought. Those stubborn counselors fought their way back, though. Nick, who would later become Fr. Nick, was an absolute ringer. Every time up, he crushed the ball for a home-run. Years later, he told me that he wanted to play pro ball. That day, his last home run had put the counselors in front by one run.

We had one last at bat. Our first two batters got out, and I stepped to the plate. Everyone was screaming. I looked at the on deck circle and saw that one of the many Marys would be batting after me. This particular Mary was very kind, very sweet, and very religious. She was the type of girl you wanted to take home to your mother, but so help me God, she could not swing a baseball bat to save her life. So, I knew that our last chance was for me to hit a homerun. As I stood at the plate, I saw how deep the outfielders were positioned. I didn't know if I could hit it over them.

The pitches started coming in. The umpire called a strike, then two balls, then another strike. One more strike, and I would be out. Both sides were screaming. I stepped out of the batter's box. I glanced over at Mary and a thought crossed my mind. The outfielders were so deep, all I had to do was connect with the ball, hit it into the outfield, and I could easily get on base. Then, Mary would come up. There was no question that she would make the last out. But at least everyone could blame Mary for the loss, not me.

Knucklehead that I am, that's what I did. I swung and connected just enough to send the ball floating into shallow right field. I ran mightily to first base and made it there safely. Then, all the attention turned to Mary.

As tiny, kind, sweet, horrible-baseball-playing Mary stepped up to the plate, the umpire literally had to remind her how to hold the bat.

I watched intently from first base as the pitcher tossed the first pitch. Mary swung and missed, but suddenly I saw the umpire rising out of his crouch and looking towards me at first base. I wondered what in the world he was looking at me for. He then pointed at me and yelled, "You're off the base! You're out! Game over!"

I'd forgotten that you couldn't lead off a base in softball. I was the final out, and the game was over. I wanted to cry. And guess who was the first person to come over and offer me a kind word? Mary. What an idiot I was. Why didn't I just take my swings?

That was one long walk back to the cabin.

I knew one thing for sure; whatever opportunities I had in life, I was going to take my swings and let the chips fall where they may.

Lesson learned: Even with painful lessons, God is always fine tuning us for the bigger victory ahead.

Chapter Eight

As I got off the elevator, in the lobby of O'Malley, Surhoff, and Kraft, I waited in a line of people who were signing out. I pulled out my cell phone and dialed Mr. Witherspoon's number. Fortunately, he picked up.

"Mr. Witherspoon, its Michael Alexopoulos. I just met with Surhoff. The best I could do is to get you one day every other month, supervised. It's not a great deal, but I recommend you take it." He didn't respond. At first, I thought he was angry that I took the deal, but then I realized we'd lost our connection. "Mr. Witherspoon? I think I'm losing you. I said the best I could do …" I realized I was practically shouting this sensitive information in the lobby, so I stopped myself. "I'm in a lobby. I'll call you when I'm outside."

I hung the phone up, and as I waited in line, I noticed the African-American security guard who was holding the door open earlier for Surhoff. Next to him, I saw the young, African-American boy, still wearing his dad's oversized security guard hat as he spun around on his stool. The security guard handed me the pen.

"Signing out, sir?" he said. I nodded as he indicated where I should sign. I couldn't help but notice the young boy proudly watching as his dad signed for a package, answered the phone, and helped everyone.

"Is that your dad?" I asked the young boy. He just smiled proudly and nodded.

"It's Follow Daddy Day at his school today," the guard said as he tousled his son's hat. "All the kids get to follow their dads around and see what they do." As I walked away, I took one more glance back at the young boy and his father. I walked outside and dialed Mr. Witherspoon's number. It rang a few times. At that very moment something happened that changed my day and my life.

I hung the phone up before Mr. Witherspoon answered.

Many times after this, I asked myself why I did that. The best answer I came up with is that there is a voice inside each of us that is undeniable. Sometimes, you just have to listen to it even when you know it will lead you down the road less traveled. The problem is, when we are young we avoid this road because we are too nervous about where it will lead us and as we grow older, we avoid it because we are simply too tired to encounter the unknown hazards that may lie ahead. In the end, a lifetime, our lifetime, has passed and all we have done is gaze down that road wondering where it would have led us. However, on this day, for whatever reason, I veered off and headed down that road.

Instead of calling Mr. Witherspoon again, I dialed Surhoff's number, and he picked up with a quizzical tone in his voice.

"Yes?"

"It's Michael Alexopoulos. Sorry to interrupt again. Listen, there is no question that the law is on your side, but ethically, morally, I think this kid deserves to be with his dad more than one day every other month. And I don't think the visits need to be supervised.

I'm just appealing to you … to give that some consideration," I said.

There was a long pause and once again, I thought my phone had gone dead. But, then I heard Surhoff's voice come through loud and clear.

"Are you still in the building?" Surhoff asked.

"No, I'm on the street. Do you want me to come up?"

"Mr. Alexis. Look up," said Surhoff. I glanced up at the mammoth building he was in. I could feel Surhoff looking at me from his glass tower like a spec on the ground beneath him.

"The next time I make you an offer, you take it and say thank you. Understand?" He paused and then dealt the deathblow. "As of now, all offers are off the table. Tell that to your client." I heard the phone click off. I stood there wondering why in God's name I made the phone call.

As Surhoff tucked his phone away, he smiled to another lawyer nearby who'd been listening.

"Why don't you throw them a bone?" the attorney asked Surhoff. "Give them a couple extra days of visitation. We don't want any trouble with this case." Surhoff dismissed him with a wave.

"We took it for free. Let's at least have a little fun with it," he said with a smile.

"I don't want to get this Alexopoulos angry at us and have it get ugly in court," the attorney said.

"Please. Michael Alexopoulos hasn't seen the inside of a courtroom since we beat him four years ago." He pulled out his reading glasses as he resumed his work and then peered over them to the attorney. "He's a toothless Tiger."

"You're sure about that?"

"I'm the one who took his teeth away," Surhoff said with a laugh. Surhoff seemed to relish this. My dad's law firm was the only firm that consistently gave him fits in court and even though I didn't work there anymore, he loved the fact that he could toy with me knowing who my dad was.

Down by the outdoor fountain, I collected my thoughts and called Mr. Witherspoon.

I relayed to him what had happened. I felt awful about it. I kept wondering if my ego had gotten the best of me. Was I really trying to do the right thing? Why didn't I just shut my mouth and get this thing over with?

"Well, what do you think is fair under the law?" Mr. Witherspoon asked me sincerely. I wanted to yell out that the words "fair" and "law" were oxymora. Fair was simply determined by the amount of money a client had.

"Mr. Witherspoon, the reality is you should have equal and joint custody of your son. But that is not going to happen. That is just not the world we live in."

"But the attorney who referred me to you spoke very highly of you Mr. Alexopoulos and said that in a trial, you were—"

I had to interrupt him, and lay it out straight. I explained to him that the reason another attorney referred him to me was that once the attorney knew that his case was a loser, he wasn't going to spend his time on it. He threw out my name, figuring he might just get a little referral money for doing nothing.

"Mr. Witherspoon, you must have been talking to someone who hasn't seen me in a long time, because I haven't been inside a courtroom in four years."

He fell silent at my honesty.

"I've become a transactional lawyer. I shuffle papers. I mean if this were a jaywalking ticket or a traffic violation, I'd be your guy. But this is your kid we are talking about, and you're going to need a formidable law firm to go up against Surhoff. I'm just not the right person for you to be talking to."

"All my filing deadlines are in two days. I won't be able to get another attorney. I'll never see my kid again." He was right. He wouldn't see his kid again.

"You're my last chance." I looked at the mammoth building that hovered above me. I wanted to say no, but I was the one who blew the offer. I had to take responsibility for it.

"Okay, Mr. Witherspoon." And that was it. With that simple okay, I had the baseball bat in my hands again and was standing at the plate. Would I have the courage to take my swings?

Chapter Nine

Jerome and I finished eating at Sophia's apartment when she enthusiastically held up a picture of a tuxedo in a men's magazine.

"What do you guys think?" she asked.

"It seems fine," I said.

"Jerome?" Sophia inquired, knowing his taste was much better than mine.

"Love it," he said with complete conviction. So, that confirmed it. We finally had our tuxes picked out.

"What about the bride's maid's dresses?" I asked.

"Well, I brought one home," she said as she pointed to it nearby. "But none of the girls could make it by tonight to try it on."

"Isn't there someone else we could get to try it on?" I asked. Sophia and I both innocently looked over to Jerome who was finishing up his dinner. He just stared back at us.

"Uh-uh, people. Don't even look over here. I'm not putting on a dress." Sophia gave him her best puppy dog eyes stare.

He looked over to me and said, "Alright, rock, paper, scissors. The loser has to wear the dress for her." Okay, I loved Sophia, but I wasn't trying on that dress.

"It's that, or you know she will be sulking all night," said Jerome. Good point, I thought. Jerome dramatically held up his fist and away we went. We pounded our fists three times on the table and made our choices. He held out his fist strongly choosing a rock, only to look over and see me holding out my palm, representing the paper. Victory was mine!

A few minutes later, the bathroom door swung open, to reveal Jerome dressed up in the stylish bride's maid dress. At least he wasn't a sore loser. He walked by us like he was a fashion model.

"I am a young bride's maid, going down the aisle of a Greek church, and I am working my bride's maid dress."

"Jerome, it's a church, not a cat walk," I said.

"Whatever," Jerome said without looking back. Sophia turned to me, looking for my opinion. "So, what do you think?"

"I like it. I think."

"Do you think the flower on the side makes his butt look big," Sophia said.

"Well, yeah," I replied.

"Okay, fashion show's over," Jerome said spinning around. Then, for good measure, he threw in some Greek to tell me to hit the road.

"Jerome, I gotta tell you. It kills me that you speak better Greek than I do," I said as he went to change in the bedroom.

"Two years in Corfu. I learned to cook and paint there too. Did I ever show you my water paintings of the hillside that I did?" I told him I'd seen them, and they were fantastic.

"Just tell me something you're bad at Jerome. Make me feel good about myself," I said laughing. One of things that I always found so endearing about Jerome was that he had grown up as a foster child. Because of his pockmarked skin and his height, people who were adopting never viewed him as a cute, cuddly kid to adopt. They missed such a great person. Eventually he aged out, a term given to children who grow older, never are adopted, and eventually head out into the world on their own. I think one of the reasons Jerome was so good at so many things was that he was always trying to please people so he could fit in somewhere with some family. But, that day never came, even as he got older. Eventually, he began working at the Lombard Foster Center as an administrator. Those kids became his family, and it was wonderful to watch him work with them. That's how Sophia met Jerome. When she was getting her internship hours to become a licensed family therapist, she volunteered at the Foster Center and they became the best of friends.

As we were cleaning up, my cell phone rang. I answered to hear my dad's secretary on the other line. She told me my dad had time to see me. I know that sounds weird, but my dad never called me directly. He always had his secretary call me. I told her I was on my way and hung up the phone. I wanted to get these problems with my mom and him over with.

"I gotta run. My dad has an opening in his schedule."

"An opening in his schedule? Is he going to charge you for the visit?" said Jerome.

"Knowing my dad, probably." I grabbed my coat and kissed Sophia goodbye. But before I could get out the door, she put her arms around me.

"One last request: when you come back, can we work on our first dance? Jerome said he'd help us. He's a dance instructor. He's great at this stuff."

"Dance instructor? He teaches spinning classes on weekends," I replied.

"Excuuuuse me! I'm not deaf in here. The dance classes are right next door to my spinning classes. I know every move!"

With that, Jerome came out with the dress partially clinging to him and started dancing up a storm. He was a great dancer, too. I should have known.

Chapter Ten

The sound of my heels clacking on the marble floor of my dad's upscale offices brought back memories of the day I was fired. I passed by the receptionist; I wasn't going to stop and get permission from her to go back and see my dad. It was weird enough coming back up to his offices and being treated like an outsider. I hadn't been there since he fired me.

I'd forgotten how beautiful his law offices were. Maybe I just hadn't noticed it before. After working in the dump Todd and I had rented, this place looked amazing.

As I walked down the hall, attorneys and receptionists who had known me for years looked the other way or gave me the slightest of nods as I walked by. I entered my Dad's office as he was getting off the phone. I didn't sit, and I didn't take off my coat. When I was starting out in law, my dad told me that you should never do these things when you walk in front of a judge or into someone's office because it tells them you are willing to wait. Today, I wasn't willing to wait. I just wanted to get this over with.

Of course my dad tried to start on some other point of interest to deflect our awkwardness. "Saw Surhoff in court today. You ready to take him on again?"

I told my dad that I didn't come to his offices to talk law. I came there to talk about him and Mom. He looked incredulous and told me he didn't want to get into that.

"I just want you to get this junk between you and Mom resolved so everything gets back to normal," I said.

"Normal?" he responded.

"Yeah, normal."

"Okay, here's the case finding: we're not in love anymore."

"You're telling me you don't love mom anymore?"

"No, no. I'll always love your mother. But whether we're in love anymore is a different story." He talked about it like he was discussing a legal brief.

"So, you're telling me you're actually going to go through with this. You're going to get a divorce?"

My dad leaned back and said that divorces were messy and costly but assured me that he'd been thinking about this and came up with the perfect way to get around this. He paused, so proud of himself that he'd found the solution.

"You," he said.

"Me?" I replied in confusion.

"Yeah. We have a one-day arbitration. You draw up the divorce settlement. You're impartial. You love us both. Who would do a better job?" With total sincerity and earnestness, he continued. "And we'll pay for your wedding."

"Is that what you called me here for?" I said.

"No, I wanted to congratulate you on your engagement to uh … uh …"

"Sophia," I said.

"Sophia, right. You brought up all this divorce stuff," my dad said.

That slip up told me everything I needed to know. He could care less about our getting married. He could barely remember Sophia's name. He just wanted to get in a room with my mother so he could vent, and he didn't want a non-partisan attorney there because it would actually cost him money.

He leaned across his desk, trying to sell his brilliant idea. "Listen, everyone wins here. You get your wedding paid for, and our divorce is amicable."

What a waste of time this was, I thought. This was just another charade. Another hoop he wanted all of us to jump through so that he could look magnanimous when he and my mom reconciled. So, I told him I would set up a time to get them together so we could get this over with and I could get on with my wedding.

As I headed out of my dad's law firm, I saw through the reflection in the mirror that my dad had gone right back to work, not missing a beat. I was just another appointment in his day.

Chapter Eleven

Sophia worked as a marriage and family therapist. She primarily saw couples who were struggling in their marriages or families with kids who had emotional problems. She was great at what she did. It seemed like such a noble profession to me, helping people resolve their personal problems so they could make it through their lives.

She worked at The Family Therapy Center. I never knew anyone who saw a therapist. If my family had a problem with someone, they tended to simply yell at that person. The other person would yell back, and then they'd sit down and eat dinner together. I suppose that was Greek therapy, and it seemed to work.

But, as I got to know and understand Sophia's work more, I began to realize that the web of a person's family structure could propel them further in life or it could restrict and immobilize them.

I arrived at Sophia's work, and the receptionist let her know. She got off the phone a few seconds later and told me to wait in the meeting room across the hall.

As I entered the meeting room, I saw a large tote board. I gazed up at it and saw a heading that read, "Genealogy Map—the Davis Family." A cobweb of family names stretched across the board. "Uncle Frank Davis and Aunt Sarah Davis—married thirteen years—divorced," "Grandfather Steve Davis and Grandmother Cathy Davis—married forty-eight years—Grandmother deceased," "Father Doug Davis and Mother Joanne Davis—twenty-two years marriage—separated—spousal abuse." All the names on the board connected down to the final pair of names on the board, "Doug Davis, Jr. and Barbara Davis—married eighteen months—separated—in counseling."

I'd never seen anything like this. This board showed everything that happened in a family that led up to the two people in the middle. Just then, Sophia entered the room.

"Hey you," she said as she came over and we exchanged a kiss. I glanced back at the board.

"What is this board for?" I asked her.

"It's a genealogy map," Sophia said. She explained to me that whenever a couple comes to them for counseling, they put a genealogy map together. It maps out their entire family history. That way they can see their family history of abuse, divorce, or whatever the problem is. Once they're aware of it, they try and help them break the cycle. Her fingers traced along the board, indicating some red flags.

"This is a make-believe one that we show couples. But you can see in this one how for generations there was alcoholism and spousal abuse. And it leads up to this couple. We try and point out that more than likely the same thing will happen to them unless they break the cycle."

I looked back at the board and studied it for a few moments. "How do they break the cycle?" I asked.

"You get them to settle their accounts," she said looking over the board.

"What does that mean?"

She ran her fingers along the generations of the past. "It means all this turmoil that's happened in their past …" she said as she pointed to the red flags along the board, "They have to acknowledge it, and then make peace with it. That's the first step in breaking the cycle."

Before I could ask any more questions, she interjected. "C'mon, I only have a half hour for lunch."

Sophia took me out to the courtyard that was adjacent to their building, and we began to eat our lunches. I told her that I took my dad up on his offer to get him and my mom together.

"You agreed to it?" she said in disbelief.

"Look, I'll get them in a room, sit down with them, put something on paper, and get them to start talking to each other. Thirty minutes later, we'll rip everything up."

"You don't think they'll go through with it?"

"Greeks don't get divorced. They'd rather live together miserably for fifty years than be embarrassed by divorce."

That is true. Growing up, I can hardly remember anyone we knew getting divorced. If someone did, it was really big news.

Chapter Twelve

What a strange moment this was, I thought as I approached the conference room in my dad's law offices and saw my parents already seated. My mother looked elegant and secure as she sat at one end of the long legal table while my dad sifted through some papers on the other side. As I took a seat at the head of the table in between them, I thought about how stupid this was.

"Okay, now, I should put you both in separate rooms and go back and forth," I said as I looked at both of them. "But, do you really want to go through with this?" Neither of them budged. And then my Dad took on a legal air.

"Proceed, counselor," he said.

"Go ahead," said my Mom.

I opened a folder of their financial assets. I knew once they started hearing the actual words, they'd come to their senses.

"Okay, I guess we'll start with the easiest asset to divide. Your bank stock," I said, "What's the current market value?"

"Worthless. Next asset," my father said in a gruff mamer.

I had barely turned to my mother when I instantly saw her react. "What? Who in the name of God do you think you're kidding?" she said. "That stock is worth at least five hundred thousand dollars," she said with her voice rising.

"Like you ever looked at it," my dad retorted.

"You're right. I didn't look at it. You know why? I was too busy cleaning the house, washing your shirts, and taking care of our kids!"

The conference room that was so quiet a moment ago suddenly became charged with tension. What I began to witness was two people who had never spoken to each other about these issues suddenly begin to let loose.

"Is that right? Let me tell you, while I was out there busting my hump, trying to build up my practice, you were busy doing other things too, weren't you?"

I knew this was spinning out of control. So, I jumped up and shut the conference room door. "Okay, wait a second ..." I said.

"You think you're any different? You think I don't know about your little escapades?" yelled my mother.

"You don't know squat, honey!" my dad yelled back.

"Don't you ever call me honey again! Don't you ever raise your voice to me again!" yelled mom.

"I will say any darn thing I please, honey. Freedom of speech, remember? Article One, amendment to the Constitution of the United States," shouted dad.

My mom had had enough, and she got up, fuming, and grabbed some soda cans that were on the table.

"You will never talk to me that way, again!" she yelled as she reared back and threw the soda cans at my dad. Dad ducked, and the cans crashed into the wall behind him, but he kept reciting the constitution.

"Congress shall make no law respecting an establishment of religion ..." continued Dad as the cans bounced around behind him.

"You can sleep with these stupid books for all I care!" she yelled as she grabbed some of his legal books and flung them at him. My dad crouched beneath the table as the books hit the chairs around him.

"... or prohibiting the free exercise thereof; or abridging the freedom of speech!" he yelled. My mom then turned and grabbed an exquisite, large glass vase.

"Hold on, Mom!" I said trying to stop her.

"I will die before you steal one penny from me!" she yelled as she held the vase up.

"That's a $ 5,000 dollar vase!" my dad said, staring in dismay that she would even think of throwing it.

"I know it is! I decorated this place, you jerk!" she yelled right as she hurled the vase at my dad who just barely made it out the door before the vase exploded against it. My mom grabbed her purse and stormed out of the room. The room looked like a bomb had gone off in it. I just stared at the mess in dismay when suddenly my cell phone rang.

"Hello," I said.

I heard Sophia's enthusiastic voice on the other end of the line. "Are you all set?"

"For what?" I replied.

"Our first marriage counseling session," she said cheerfully.

"Oh, right."

"You don't sound excited."

"No, no, I'm really excited," I said as I stared at the decimated room.

I told her I would be there shortly, then hung the phone up and sat there as the reality of the situation came into full focus. My parents were getting divorced and all of our lives would be irrevocably changed.

Chapter Thirteen

I sat in my car at the church parking lot trying to collect my thoughts before I went in for our first marital counseling session. A few moments later, Sophia pulled up in the spot next to mine. I got out of the car and greeted her. Before going in, I told Sophia about my parents. We sat outside for a few minutes, both trying to process everything. How would it change all of our lives? How would it change our wedding? Before we got too far, Fr. Jim showed up, and we told him the news. I really wasn't sure how he'd react or what he'd say, but he simply looked at me and said, "I'm so sorry." He didn't ask for details or ask me who was at fault. He just put me at ease.

He opened his office, and we went inside. What should have been a happy first session seemed to be so heavy all of a sudden.

"Divorce is rough, no two ways about it," Fr. Jim said. "Listen, I'm in the life and death business, and I can tell you there is only one thing worse than death. That's divorce." He readjusted his seat before carrying on. "Death—you cry, you miss the person, you think about all the good things they did for you. Divorce … it's like a bomb goes off and every child, aunt, uncle, and friend who is anywhere near the divorcing couple gets hit by it." He went to his filing cabinet and pulled out a folder and some leaflets about marriage.

"That's why we do these sessions. We don't want you to end up another statistic. So over the next few weeks, I'll be asking you a lot of questions. I want to make sure you're headed in the right direction."

I took the pamphlets from him, but my thoughts were elsewhere. When the day began, I felt like Sophia and I were coming in for a routine marriage checkup, but now because of my parents' situation, everything had changed. I felt as though I was suddenly carrying the dreaded divorce gene. I could see it in all of our demeanors and in everyone's face. Somehow, I knew that Sophia felt that her fear of bad things happening to people she was close to was coming to fruition. We wrapped up our counseling session, and Sophia and I headed out.

As we walked back to our cars, I told Sophia that I wanted to check in with my mom. I kissed her goodnight and drove over to my mom's house, which was nearby.

As I walked in to my parents' house, my mom was packing whatever personal items my dad had left behind in several boxes. Legal briefs, tax returns, desk lamps: she was cramming everything hurriedly into random boxes.

"He was married to his law firm, Michael. He spent more time there than he did with me. What kind of a life is that? His work ruined his relationship with you, your sister, and now me."

"Dad made it sound like you were having an affair ..." I said quietly.

"Michael, I was a woman in the prime of my life, and he was treating me like I was one of his employees. Do this, say that, smile. I had needs, and he wasn't meeting those needs. And I'll be darned if I was going to let my … my spirit, my soul, my love just rot away."

She tossed some of his legal books into another box and closed it. "It wasn't an affair, Michael. It was companionship. It was taking a cooking class. It was talking about a *Times* bestseller book. It was appreciating a sunset. It wasn't physical; it was just companionship."

I understood what she was saying, but it was still painful to hear. It hurts to learn that your parents were unfaithful to each other. Until you live through it, you don't realize how much damage infidelity causes. We live in a culture that makes it sound like it really isn't so bad. We now call an affair an "indiscretion." I can tell you first hand, affairs are not indiscretions, they are family destroyers. They are life-altering tragedies, and they are generation cripplers that leave a wound on every friend and relative who surrounds your family.

I remembered back to an incident, several years before. My dad and I were watching a TV show about President Kennedy and his alleged affairs with other women. I asked my dad why weren't people outraged that Kennedy did that to his wife, and he said, "He never embarrassed her. He kept everything quiet." In some weird way, I felt as if my dad was saying to me, "As long as you don't embarrass your wife, it's okay to have affairs."

"When did all this start?" I asked my mom.

"It built up over the years. It's just taken this long for me to stand my ground."

"I never wanted you kids in the middle of this. So, if you don't want to draw up the settlement, I understand. But, I'll tell you this ... if you want to draw it up, I'll look at it. If I like it, your father can take it or leave it. Period."

I told her I would draw up the settlement. As I made my way out of my parents' house, I couldn't believe how lifeless it felt. This was our home where we shared so many laughs, so much love, so many memories, but suddenly it seemed as though, like a thief, the vagaries of life had entered our house and had stolen all the joy it possessed.

I got into my car and slowly wound through a backed-up Eisenhower Freeway. It was probably the only time the traffic didn't bother me because it gave me a chance to think.

I approached a tollbooth and took out my wallet to pay the toll. I saw the tattered paper icon of the Archangel Michael that I had gotten at church camp so many years ago sticking out of one of the pockets in my wallet. I pulled it out and flipped it over. I could still make out the words, "Who is God?" printed on the back of the icon.

As I sped back up and rejoined the rush hour traffic, I thought about that icon and how it taught me that God was a God of order and that He had a purpose for each of us. When you are a young child, it is easier to believe that such order exists. After all, your life is in order when you are a kid. School, play time, bed time. Summers. Holidays. Everything is structured and ordered. When you are done with school, and you head out into the real world, life just gets more chaotic. I know it did for me. I yearned to know my own individual purpose. But as the years ticked by, I lost faith that God really had a purpose for me.

From the freeway, I could see St. Basil Greek Orthodox Church. I made the sign of the cross over my chest as a sign of veneration, just as I had been taught. But I couldn't help but think, "Where are you God?"

A couple of years earlier, when my dad fired me, I pretty much lost everything I had. I lost my job, my house, my car, and the girl I was going to marry who left me. I remember praying in my house, the night before I lost it. It wasn't a casual, do your cross before bed prayer. It was a down on my knees, "I need your help" prayer. I just wanted to know He was still there and watching over me. I prayed as hard as I'd ever prayed that night for some sign, some glimpse that I was still on God's radar. Where was I to go with my life? How was I going to regroup? I just needed some guidance from Him as to where He wanted me to go with my life. And for days, I kept looking for a sign. You know the only thing that happened that week? Todd Klinger called me. We hadn't seen each other in awhile, and he wanted to know if I would be willing to split some office space with him because he couldn't afford the monthly rent.

That was it. That was God's interest level in me. No other firm that I'd sent out my resumes to was interested in hiring me. My dad didn't call with a change of heart. Despina Konaris didn't call and say she'd overreacted. Nothing like that happened. I just got a call from Todd saying he'd like to split office space.

I took the office space and thought that somewhere in there God had a purpose for me. But, two years later, Todd and I were still struggling to pay our office bills, and my journey in life was weakening. This was no answer from God. It felt like me grasping at straws.

I never thought, "Why me?" as though God was doing this to me. Instead, I felt like

God had gone silent, as though He had simply forgotten about me. For some reason, I didn't hold His interest anymore.

When I was on top, God always seemed to be there: everything clicked, and I'd say, "Thank God" to give Him the credit. But now, God seemed to be nothing more than a fair-weather friend to me.

So, after all this time, I finally had fallen back in love and was slowly regrouping my life. Then my parents announced their divorce just as I was about to get married. The one area of my life where there was a ray of sun, God put a cloud over it. It felt like I was just getting back on my feet and God kicked the stool out from under me.

I thought back to when I was a little kid, Greek dancing across the floor for my parents and wanting those three precious things in life: my culture, my family, and God.

As I drove along, I couldn't help but feel that I was losing them all.

Robert Krantz

What I learned at Church Camp – Lesson #4

"Loss is difficult."

Loss is difficult. This was one of the toughest lessons I learned at camp that summer. Even today, I have to ask myself if this really happened as I remember it. But, the details are clear. This is the way it happened.

One afternoon, all the campers were near the swimming pool, just goofing around. Suddenly, we heard a piercing clang. It lasted for only a few seconds and stopped, but something told all of us that something bad had happened. You could just feel it in the air. All of us started running quickly towards the sound in hopes that it was inconsequential. But, it wasn't. As we got closer to the laundry room, everyone stopped running and several of the adult counselors told us what had happened. A young man who worked at the campsite had reached into one of the large washers, and it tore his arm off from the elbow down. They had quickly gotten him into a car and were speeding away towards the hospital. But he was bleeding badly, and the hospital was far away.

Some of the campers started crying. Others started praying. I heard someone say that Mr. Kanavas had retrieved the portion of the young man's arm and was headed towards the lunch hall. At that exact moment, something that my mother had told me crossed my mind: that if someone ever lost a limb, you should put it in salt water. Even to this day I wonder, what made my mother tell me that? Greek parents are protective of their kids, but this went way beyond shouting, "*Ta matia tessera!*" (Have four eyes, two in front and two in back!) as we ran out the door.

When did she say this to me, I later wondered? Was I leaving for school one day? "Did you clean your ears? Did you tie your shoes? Okay, good. Make sure you look both ways when you cross the street … and by the way, if anybody should lose a limb today, make sure you put it in salt water."

I began running at full speed towards the lunch hall. I saw Mr. Kanavas entering it from the back. He had covered the arm with a white cloth and was looking for something to place it in so he could take it to the hospital. I can still remember Mr. Kanavas' face—how strong he was. I yelled out to him to put it in salt water to preserve it. He never said a word to me. At first, I didn't think he wanted to be bothered by a young camper. But, as he filled a large white pail with water, he reached over and grabbed a box of salt. He tipped it over; I can still see the entire contents of that saltbox pouring into the pail with the arm and water in it. Once it was full, he whipped out the back, got in his car, and raced towards the hospital.

I'd never heard of anyone being able to reattach an arm in those days, but we were at a church camp and I was absolutely convinced that God would make a miracle happen. Fr. Angelo called us into the chapel and led us in prayer. We first prayed that the young man wouldn't die from all the blood he'd lost. We prayed for the doctors. We prayed that God would help them reattach his arm. We prayed, and we prayed.

Later that evening Fr. Angelo called us into the church hall. He was very calm and told us that the young man was fine, but that the doctors could not save his arm. I could hear the air sucked out of all of the campers. All of us truly believed that God would reattach this young man's arm. How could this happen? He was working at a church camp. What had he done to deserve this? It was weird to read about all the miracles Jesus did: healing one person, resurrecting another. I couldn't help but think about the young worker. Why couldn't Jesus help him?

Fr. Angelo must have sensed how crushed we were, because a few days later he sat us all down in the chapel and said, "Sometimes 'no' is an answer from God. And for whatever reason God did not allow this man to have his arm reattached. Now, we have to pray for God to help him to cope with his loss. I know it doesn't seem like it, but even when we lose, God is still working."

Fr. Angelo's words were comforting, but honestly I viewed God differently after that day. Loss is difficult.

Lesson learned: Even when we've lost and are at our lowest, God is still working.

Chapter Fourteen

There were several young women outside of our offices, filling out some paperwork and chewing gum as I walked up. It looked like they were waiting to audition for their high school play.

"Can I help you?" I asked.

"We're interviewing for the secretary job."

"The secretary job?" I replied. I walked into our offices and saw Todd and Stan there.

"What did I miss?"

"Dena quit. She got a better job."

"She didn't even give us any notice?"

"No. We've got to interview those girls after our meeting."

Treete, I thought. *Treete* basically means three in Greek. It's a Greek superstition that bad news comes in threes. First I messed up on Surhoff's offer to Mr. Witherspoon, then my parents got divorced, and now Dena quit. At least the bad news was over. So, with some hope, I turned to Todd.

"How'd the Witherspoon hearing go this morning?"

The judge had asked a psychologist to determine whether Mr. Witherspoon's son was mature enough to be a witness during the proceedings. We had asked the judge to allow us to have a jury trial, and I felt the child testifying could connect with jurors who might feel sympathetic towards him.

"The psychologist said its okay for his kid to testify and the judge allowed us to have a jury trial," said Todd.

Finally, some good news. It turned out that Texas was one of the few remaining states that allowed a jury trial in child custody cases. Because the case had been transferred up from Texas, the judge allowed us to have a jury on the case. Maybe there was something to that *treete* superstition. As we walked towards the conference room, I pulled Stan to the side, thinking this would be a good time to set him up with my sister.

"Hey, Stan … do you have any plans for this Friday night?" He thought about it for a moment.

"No, I think it's open," he said.

"I wanted all of us to get together and go over the case. I thought we'd meet over at my mom's house … you know, give us some room to stretch out," I told him, trying not to sound too obvious.

"Sure" he said, oblivious to my plans to set him up with my sister.

"My mom, my *yia yia* … and my sister … will be there, you know, just hanging out … so you may want to wear something nice."

"Yeah, yeah. No problem."

Todd happened to hear me as he walked by. He rolled his eyes at my matchmaking efforts. As I passed by him, I leaned back and said, "Hey, do you want to get this curse off of us or not?"

"Us? What do you mean us? The curse includes law partners?" Todd said nervously.

"I don't know. I gotta check with my *yia yia* on that one," I said with a smile.

As we walked into the conference room, Mr. Witherspoon was staring at a picture someone had taken many years ago of Todd and me dancing with our briefcases in our hands outside a courthouse.

"Good news Mr. Witherspoon," I said. "The court psychologist told the judge it would be okay for your son to testify. Judges almost always follow what the psychologist recommends."

"That's great," said Mr. Witherspoon.

"And the judge allowed us to have a jury trial. All of this will help us."

I motioned to Stan, "This is Stan Nichols. He'll be helping us with jury selection." Stan and Mr. Witherspoon shook hands as Todd and I went to get some sodas out and put them on the conference table.

Mr. Witherspoon motioned back to the picture of Todd and me dancing outside of a courthouse. "Is that you two?"

I turned to the picture. It had been awhile since I really looked at it. "Yeah, it seems like a long time ago," I said. Stan read the caption underneath the picture:

TWO LOCAL ATTORNEYS CELEBRATE A VICTORY
IN THEIR MOOT COURT CASE.

"That must have been a big case you won," said Mr. Witherspoon.

"Actually, it was just for school. It was a mock trial that we'd won."

Mr. Witherspoon laughed out loud when he heard this. "What were you celebrating so hard for?"

"Well …" I turned to Todd, "What were we celebrating for?"

Todd looked at the picture and said, "We won."

Mr. Witherspoon still smiling at us, "Do you fellas still dance like that after every case you win?"

"No, no," I said quickly.

"Yeah, no more dancing for us," chimed in Todd.

There was a slight laugh from everyone, and then Todd and I sat down at the conference table. I doubt they realized it, but it was an awkward moment for Todd and me. We used to love practicing law. That's all we ever talked about. Law. Legal cases. Lawyers:

Gerry Spence, Vincent Bugliosi, David Boies. We wanted to be like the great ones. We loved it, and it showed in that picture. But, the years had taken away that enthusiasm. We rarely talked about law anymore. Instead, we talked about paying bills and getting by.

As we began to prep Mr. Witherspoon for his deposition, I couldn't help but steal one more glance at the picture of Todd and me dancing on the sidewalk. I wondered what happened to those guys.

Chapter Fifteen

"How did you and Michael meet?" asked Fr. Jim as he began our weekly counseling session in his church offices.

"We've known each other since we were kids and dated up through high school."

"What happened then?"

"When I was nineteen, my dad died … and I went through a bad time. I stopped seeing Michael."

"How did your Dad die?"

"A heart attack. We had gone out to get ice cream after a softball game. And on the way home, he said he wasn't feeling good, and suddenly he slumped over. I pulled the car over … I did everything I could … but he died."

Sophia did do everything she could on that day, but she always felt that if someone else had been there, they could have saved him. It simply wasn't true. Her dad died within seconds of having his heart attack. There was nothing she or anyone else could have done.

"You said that's when things broke off between you. What happened?"

"She cut off everyone, including me. And she …" my voice trailed off.

"I got really messed up."

"I kept trying to see her, and she just kept saying how much she hated me. She was in college at the time and didn't want any part of me."

"Why were you mad at Michael?"

"Displaced anger. I hated the world." Sophia took a sip of water before continuing. "About a year later, I got married to someone I'd known for seven months."

"So you've been married before?"

"Yeah. I was divorced within a year. My life … I was pretty messed up."

"And what were you doing at this time?" Fr. Jim asked as he glanced back to me.

"I was working for my dad's law firm. After a couple years, I started dating Despina

Konaris. Everyone always thought we were the perfect Greek couple. Eventually, we got engaged. My life seemed perfect. I was making a lot of money working for my dad, and then came the Blue Steel case."

"What was that?"

"That was one of the biggest law suits my dad's firm had ever tried. O'Malley, Surhoff, and Kraft were the defense attorneys. My Dad let me be lead counsel."

"What happened?"

"We had the case won. All I had to do was make a decent closing and ... I blew it. It cost the firm a lot of money. My dad was furious. He called me into the office and in front of everyone ... he fired me," I said. "I pretty much lost everything after that. Despina and I broke up. I lost my home. I basically had to start back from zero."

Fr. Jim smiled, "Okay, so how in the world did you two ever reconnect?"

We laughed at his question, and it broke the mood for a moment. Sophia told him that for years she refused to talk to anybody about her dad dying. She didn't think it would do any good. It wasn't going to bring him back.

"So, I kept everything inside. One night, I couldn't carry the pain anymore. I called my friend Jerome, and I just started crying and everything came out. I just couldn't understand how a God who was supposed to be so loving could do that to my dad and my family."

Fr. Jim nodded and listened closely to what she was saying.

"Finally, Jerome told me I should write a letter to God and tell him everything I felt. And I did. I wrote everything in that letter. And then we burned the letter," she said. "And then Jerome asked me, if there was anyone else that I needed to write a letter to. And I thought of Michael. I was so sorry for what I'd done to him. So, I wrote him a letter. And I told him how much I had loved him, and how sorry I was for what I'd done."

She said that when she went to therapy she learned that when bad things happen in our lives, we oftentimes disassociate ourselves with people we knew during that time because they will always remind us of that difficult period of our life.

"Did you burn that letter, too?" asked Fr. Jim.

"I was about to, but something told me to send it. Only, I didn't know where to send it," she said laughing. She explained that it had been many years since we'd spoken, and she didn't know where I lived, but she'd heard that I worked for my dad's law firm. So, she sent the letter there.

"And you got it?" he said turning to me.

"Yeah. My dad had just fired me. I was probably at my lowest point when I got the letter from Sophia. So, I called her. That was a couple years ago."

"And now you're getting married?" Fr. Jim asked.

"Yeah," I said.

"And your parents are getting divorced?"

I nodded and Fr. Jim took off his glasses and laughed, which made both of us laugh.

"Okay, this is going to be an interesting one," he said as he laughed again. "You know, it is a mystery to me sometimes how

God works. Sometimes I can see it clear as day, and sometimes it is simply blurry," he said before smiling and continuing. "This one is blurry. But I can tell you this: God is at work."

I'm glad he felt that way because in listening to our story, it sounded like we were two discarded toys that ended up on Misfit Island, clinging to each other.

Chapter Sixteen

Yia Yia Penelope was sitting at the kitchen table folding the party favors for the wedding. The party favors were *koufeta* (almonds coated with a hard white candy coating) that she carefully bundled into a sheath cloth and tied with a ribbon.

For some reason, *koufeta* is a huge deal at Greek weddings. It is kind of crazy. The almonds don't taste that great and the covering darn near cracks your teeth. However, you could walk into many a Greek house, open a drawer, and see a collection of *koufeta* from weddings spanning several generations. Some people collect coins. Others collect stamps. Greeks? We collect *koufeta* favors.

Invariably, when someone is preparing for a wedding, a *yia yia* will say, "Remember the koufeta at the Poulos wedding?" She will quietly go to an old drawer and very carefully pull out the *koufeta* from that wedding, and everyone will go, "Ooh, yeah, wow, hmm." Never mind that the couple is now divorced. It's more important that they had unique *koufeta*.

A moment later there was a knock at the front door. *Yia Yia* glanced up at the clock and shook her head slightly. Sophia was not late. She was actually right on time.

"Come on in, Sophia." Sophia entered the room with a surprised look on her face.

"How did you know it was me?"

"You're never a minute late," *Yia Yia* said ruefully. She gave Sophia some materials so she could start putting the *koufeta* in pouches. As Sophia sat down, she crossed her leg. *Yia Yia* Penelope glanced over and saw the tattoo above Sophia's ankle. It was of a face with its tongue sticking out as though it were giving someone a "raspberry." *Yia Yia* just couldn't help herself.

"May I ask you what were you thinking to have a tattoo put on your body?"

"Which one?"

"You have more than one?"

Robert Krantz

"Yeah, I've got one here, too." Sophia started to pull down her waistline.

"No, no, no. That's okay. I'll take your word for it," said *Yia Yia*.

"Well, the one on my ankle ... when I was growing up, I had a beautiful life all planned out in my mind. But that life never happened. I spent so many years trying so hard to make my beautiful life happen. One day, I realized, I had to give up trying to find that perfect life and just say ..." She did a raspberry, just like the one on her ankle and laughed at her own actions.

"You know what I mean? Now when I try and make everything perfect, I just look down there and it's like ..." She did a raspberry again.

"That is what you were thinking?"

"Yeah. You wanna know about the other one?"

"Maybe another time."

Sophia started to fold up the almonds and cloth. "So, what kind of party favors are these?" she asked.

"They're called *koufeta*. We put these almonds in a cloth and people take them home from the wedding and put them underneath their pillows."

"Wow, what's the thought process, there?" Sophia asked.

"It's a Greek superstition," said *Yia Yia*.

"I should have known," said Sophia. *Yia Yia* explained to Sophia that years ago, the priest used to dip almonds in honey and give them to the bride and groom. The hardness of the almond represented the endurance of the marriage, and the honey represented the sweetness of the marriage. The almonds were shaped like an egg, which represented fertility.

Yia Yia placed the wrapped almonds on a nearby silver tray that had two beautifully ornate crowns placed on it. She explained that they put the *koufeta* on the tray with the couple's wedding crowns, and the priest blesses them. It is believed that if a woman puts a single almond from the tray under her pillow, she'll dream of the man she's going to marry that night.

"That's neat. I like your superstitions," said Sophia.

"We always put seven almonds in each bundle."

"Why seven?"

"It's indivisible," she said. "Just like the bride and groom should be."

They each folded a few in silence. Then, Sophia asked *Yia Yia* if she worried about her marrying Michael. *Yia Yia* was honest and told her she had concerns. Sophia asked why she was concerned.

"Do you know how I got married?" asked *Yia Yia*. "My brothers sent me a note that said, 'Stavros Mitsalakis is coming to America. He's a good man, and he'll provide for you.' That was it. And you know how long we stayed married? Forty-eight years. Until the day he died. Was it easy? God, no. He could be stubborn. He could be chauvinistic. He was a real tough guy. But we learned to love each other. And when we went through tough times, we hung in there with each other."

Yia Yia told her a Greek saying. "It means, go into marriage with your eyes wide open … but once you're married, keep them half shut."

"I'm not going to be a doormat for my husband," said Sophia.

"I wasn't a doormat," said *Yia Yia*. "If he got out of line, I told him about it. That's not what I'm saying. I'm all for what you girls have going for you these days. I like that you can speak your mind, you can work if you want, dress how you like. But there is a responsibility that comes with that. You kids today: everything is disposable. Your cameras, your food, your contact lenses: you're done with them, throw them away, and get a new one. And that's how you treat your relationships. They're not working; throw them away. Try another one. And you're leaving behind all these broken families. These kids today, they're growing up, one day they go to sleep in dad's house, the next three in mom's, then back to dad's, now dad's girlfriend is spending the night while the child sleeps in the next room. It's crazy. And people wonder why these kids are all screwed up."

"And you think the same thing is going to happen to Michael and me?" Sophia asked.

"I don't see you making any attempt to get closer to him—to find out anything about his culture, because that's a big part of who he is."

Yia Yia went over to a shelf and pulled out a picture of me when I was a teenager, dancing with a circle of friends at a wedding. She showed it to Sophia.

"Michael doesn't speak Greek too good. He doesn't know Greek history that much, and he doesn't know anything about Greek politics. But let me tell you, he has the soul of a Greek. That's who he is. And if you don't understand what that is all about, you'll never be that close to Michael."

Yia Yia carefully put the picture back up on the shelf before she continued speaking.

"And he's a nice boy. He's not going to force you to be part of that culture. But ten, fifteen, twenty years from now I'll be gone, his mom and dad will be gone, and he's going to start wanting to reconnect with his roots—his heritage—and you're not going to like it, because you won't feel like you're part of it. It will cause problems between you two."

"I love that Michael embraces his culture. And I'd love to know about the history and the dances and the food … everything … but there are things that have happened in my past … Sometimes it takes me some time to get close to people."

Yia Yia softened, put her hand over Sophia's, and told her she understood. She told her that when she lost my *Papou* Stavros, she crawled into a shell, but she regretted it now.

"I should have made new friends. I should've forced myself to get out, learned to drive a car, learned about these computers. I should have kept moving. Now, look at me. I'm not much use to anybody."

"You would be a lot of help to me. Do you think you could teach me some things?"

"With open arms."

"You don't think all the relatives will make fun of me if I don't do things just right?"

Yia Yia did her version of the raspberry. "You are doing it for Michael, not for them. And he'll love you for it." Then, *Yia Yia* leaned over to Sophia. "And if anyone ever makes fun of you, you give me their name; *Yia Yia* will have a little talk with them."

Sophia looked up, somewhat at a loss. "I don't know what to learn first," said Sophia.

"Pick anything," said *Yia Yia*.

Then a smile crossed over Sophia's face. "Anything?"

Yia Yia nodded and Sophia smiled broadly.

"The superstitions," Sophia said with a wink.

Chapter Seventeen

All of the *yia yias*—and I mean *all* the *yia yias*—had gathered over at Sophia's apartment. It was a summit meeting like no other. It was like a gathering of the heads of all the Godfather families. They even got my sister Angie to show up as an interpreter for Sophia.

A *yia yia* spoke out and told Sophia a superstition in Greek. *Yia Yia* Penelope translated: "She said, 'Never step over a child. The child will stop growing.'"

"What if I do it by accident?"

"Step back over the child, they'll start growing again." All the *yia yias* nodded in agreement as they listened intently.

Then another *yia yia* chimed in, "If your hands itch, you'll be getting money soon."

"No, no, no," *Yia Yia* Penelope said, correcting her. "If your left hand itches, you'll be getting money. If your right hand itches, you're going to be giving someone money." That got more nods from the *yia yias*. Angie interpreted the next one.

"Never whistle in the dark," said Angie.

"Never!" said another *yia yia*.

"Never," confirmed another.

"Never," said one last *yia yia*.

"Why," asked Sophia innocently? *Yia Yia* Penelope asked the *yia yias* in Greek. No one really seemed to know why.

"Just … uh … don't do it, okay?" one *yia yia* finally said.

"Right. Don't do it."

"Don't do it," said one more *yia yia*.

"Don't do it," said another emphatically.

"What else?" said *Yia Yia* Penelope. A *yia yia* placed a knife on the table in front of Sophia.

"Not sure I'm going to like this one."

"Never hand somebody a knife directly," said *Yia Yia* Penelope as all the other *yia yias* nodded solemnly.

"You put like *thiiis*. On the table. Theeen, they pick up," a *yia yia* said as she demonstrated.

"If they hand it directly to you, you will get into an argument with them."

"Big-a fight."

"Enemies." All the *yia yias* nodded in agreement. There was a slight pause before *Yia Yia* brought up the one that was on everyone's mind. "Okay, what about the big one?" she said. Everyone knew what was coming.

"*Toh Mati*," all the *yia yias* said together.

"The evil eye," said Angie, translating for Sophia.

"What is that?" asked Sophia. *Yia Yia* leaned across the table to Sophia so she wouldn't miss a syllable. "When someone gives you a compliment— your children are so beautiful, you look great, what a beautiful house—be careful, they could be putting a curse on you," said *Yia Yia*.

"Only if they have brown eyes," chimed in another *yia yia*.

"Yeah, only brown eyes. So, when some-one with brown eyes gives you a compliment … you know what you do?"

"No," said Sophia.

"Spit," said *Yia Yia* Penelope.

"Spit?"

"Three times." *Yia Yia* Penelope spit quickly three times. All the other *yia yias* did the same thing right away.

"What does that do," asked Sophia?

"When you spit on something, it makes the evil spirit think, 'How special can this thing be? They're spitting on it,' and he'll leave it alone."

"That's-a right," confirmed another *yia yia*.

"Go ahead. Practice your spit," said *Yia Yia* Penelope. Sophia gave it a try. A bit too much spit went everywhere. *Yia Yia* Penelope showed her the perfect three spits. Sophia tried again. More spit. Not quite getting it. Another *yia yia* showed her with exquisite form. Sophia tried again. More spitting. Now all the *yia yias* were joining in, everyone was spitting. There couldn't be an evil spirit within a hundred miles. Just then, there was a loud knock on the door! Everyone jumped a mile high.

"It's the devil!" exclaimed one *yia yia*. Slowly, one of the *yia yias* peered out the door. Her eyes went wide.

"It's Fr. Jim!" All the *yia yias* started scrambling to clear up the spit on the table.

"I forgot, he's blessing the house today," said *Yia Yia* Penelope." She then winked at Sophia and said, "We cover all bases."

Finally, after a moment, *Yia Yia* opened the door for Fr. Jim. As he walked in, all the *yia yias* were now innocently playing cards—like some scene out of the prohibition era.

"Hi, Father Jim," the *yia yias* said in unison.

Fr. Jim knew something was up. He slowly walked over to the table. He glanced down at it and wiped up some of the leftover spittle. He glanced over to the *yia yias* who looked at him innocently.

"*Yia yia*-theology. It's gonna be the death of me," he said as he began to pull out his vestments to bless the house.

Yia Yia Penelope winked at Sophia who smiled back at her. Fr. Jim didn't have to worry about my *yia yia*. She was tight with God. I knew this for a fact: I'd seen *yia yia* pray.

What I learned at Church Camp – Lesson #5

"I saw Yia Yia praying."

One day at the camp, it was *Yia Yia*'s Day. All of the campers had their *yia yias* come up to the camp and visit. *Yia Yia* Penelope came, and it was great to see her. She seemed to know almost every *yia yia* there. I showed her all the things we'd been learning, and I could tell it meant a lot to her.

That night all the *yia yias* cooked dinner for the campers and counselors. I'm not sure, but I believe that is the day that the phrase, "too many cooks in the kitchen" originated. As happy as the *yia yias* were to be around each other, it was a known fact that none of them were going to give away any of their secret recipes. If one *yia yia* visited another and told her how much she liked her entrée or desert, the other would tell her exactly how she'd made it. But, she would always be sure to leave out one key ingredient, just so it never tasted quite as good.

Also, a *yia yia* might tell you she put three cups of sugar in a recipe, but everyone knows that *yia yias* never measured anything. All the ingredients were estimated by hand: a handful of this, a pinch of that. That way, no one could ever really duplicate a *yia yia's* recipe.

At the camp kitchen, each one of them had their corner of the kitchen cordoned off, preparing their specialty with one eye on the food and the other making sure no one was out to steal their recipe.

What a meal they prepared for us! Afterwards, the campers read some poems for them, and then we headed off to our cabins. Each *yia yia* got to stay with her grandchild. I made sure that *Yia Yia* Penelope knew where everything was, and then I told her I was going to sleep because it had been a long day. I was out cold the minute my head hit the pillow.

A few hours later, I awoke to someone talking. It sounded like someone was having a phone conversation. But, after a moment, I remembered there were no phones in the room. I listened for a moment and could tell the person was speaking Greek. I slowly got out of bed and looked across the way. There was a wood panel divider that separated my part of the room from *Yia Yia's* part of the room. As I got closer to the panels, I peeked through them. The lights were turned off, but the moon illuminated the room through a glass window at the front of the cabin. There was *Yia Yia* Penelope, on the floor, head bowed, praying. What was so amazing to me was that she was actually having a conversation with God. After every point she made, she made the sign of the cross, as if to finish that point and go onto the next. Sometimes she smiled, sometimes she cried, but for a large portion of it, she simply talked to God.

I didn't want to interrupt her, so I quietly went back to my bed and fell back asleep, but that image of her talking to God never left me. For the first time in my life, I think I really understood what prayer meant.

Lesson learned: God is listening.

Chapter Eighteen

As the tram rumbled along, I made my way to my seat, put my briefcase down, and began to stare out the window. My mind went back to the genealogy chart I saw at Sophia's workplace. I took out a sheet of paper and began making my own rough genealogy map. As I filled in Sophia's side of the paper with her relatives' names, I noticed that I was writing in the word "divorced" several times. On my side, I now had to write the word divorced by my parents' names. I wrote it too over Sophia's name for her short marriage. Seeing so many divorces in black and white in our families' histories was sobering.

I tucked the sheet away, as the tram came to a stop. I exited, along with a few other passengers. I made my way out of the terminal and walked a few blocks over to a sidewalk along the lakefront.

As part of our counseling sessions, we had to meet individually with Fr. Jim and today was one of my days to do so.

He could only fit in our session during his lunch break. So, he asked if I minded if we took a walk along the lakefront so he could get some fresh air.

I saw him waiting for me as he looked out at the boats passing by. We exchanged hellos and began to walk. Somehow, walking with the blue sky above us and the fresh air around us made the conversation easier.

"My parents were my insurance ticket. No matter how many other parents got divorced, I knew my parents would always stay married," I said.

"And what effect do you think their divorce is going to have on you and Sophia?"

"I feel like I've got to figure out what went wrong with my parents' marriage, so I can get on with my marriage with Sophia."

"Why do you think that?"

I said a Greek saying him in Greek, "The apple doesn't fall far from the apple tree." He smiled, and I continued, "You know … you come from a divorced family, your chances of getting divorced are a lot higher. There's a reason for that. It means you're carrying some kind of baggage and eventually it hurts your marriage."

"What baggage do you think you're bringing into your marriage?" Fr. Jim asked.

We stopped walking for a moment, as I thought about his question. Up until the night I knew my parents were getting divorced, I really hadn't thought about what baggage I was bringing into my marriage. "I guess that's what I've got to figure out."

"And what about Sophia? What baggage do you think she's bringing into the marriage?" I shrugged my shoulders.

"Everybody brings baggage into a marriage, Michael," he said. "The thing you have to remember is this. It's like you and Sophia are walking down a long aisle with a shopping cart between you, and you get to pick all the things you loved about your parents' relationships—the way they talked to each other, the way they held hands when no one was looking, the way they said 'I love you' before going to sleep—whatever it may be, and you get to put those great qualities in your shopping cart." He then stopped and turned towards me to make sure I got his last point.

"And all the junk. The stuff you didn't like about their relationships. That's what you leave up on the shelves."

Chapter Nineteen

I walked into our law offices and went to get my messages from our new secretary. "Hi, do I—"

"Hold it," said the new secretary, cutting me off before I could speak. She dramatically held up her hand silencing me as she finished writing some notes. I went to speak again.

"Hold it," she said. She finished writing and pointed to me. "Okay, go."

"I'm Michael. I work here. I just need my messages."

"Okay, I know I put them somewhere." She started patting various stacks of paper on her desk. Oh, brother, I thought.

"Just let me know when you find them," I said and turned towards Todd who was on the phone in his office. I covertly motioned to him to get rid of the new secretary, which made him smile. Just then, Stan walked out of the bathroom.

"Hey, Stan. Don't forget, we're meeting at my mom's tonight."

"I'm not sure I can make it. I think I'm catching a little cold." Alarm bells went off in my head. I may not have believed in these superstitions, but I didn't want to tempt the hands of fate, either.

"What do you mean? C'mon Stan, this is an important meeting." He didn't seem to be budging, as he continued to tell me he was feeling sick. So I had to resort to bribery.

"Listen, my sister makes great *avgolemono* soup (lemon and egg soup). I'll get you a big bowl of it; it'll knock out any cold you've got, okay?"

"*Avgolemono* soup. That does sound good. Okay, I think I can make it by." Whew. Thank goodness.

So my sister couldn't cook to save her life, and I'd have to ask *Yia Yia* to make the *avgolemono* soup. I had to do what I had to do to get him there. The only downside was that *Yia Yia* would now know that I was trying to set up Angie. I'm not saying my *yia yia* couldn't keep a secret. I'm just saying she liked to talk a lot to the other *yia yias*.

As I walked into my mom's house through the garage that night, I saw *Yia Yia's* unopened computer box was now plopped down collecting dust. She wasn't even using it as a prayer stool anymore. I picked it up and carried it inside.

I walked to *Yia Yia's* room. She was under the covers, watching television. "Hi, *Yia Yia*, this was in the garage."

"How did that happen?" she said innocently. I put the computer back in her room.

"I'm not letting you off the hook that easy. This thing will make you feel like you're a kid again." She smiled at my ribbing.

"I made the *avgolemeno* soup. It's good. The *gambro* will love it."

Oh, man, she was already calling Stan the "husband." She motioned for me to come closer. "Your mom told me you're having trouble finding a secretary."

"Yeah, we're still interviewing. We'll find somebody." *Yia Yia* tilted the light so she could see me better.

"Let *Yia Yia* look at you." She always did this, ever since I was a kid. It was like her version of a lie-detector test. She would give you the once-over and if there was something going on in your life, it was like she could tell it just by looking at you.

"You're losing weight," she said with concern. I could have looked like a Sumo wrestler and *Yia Yia* would have thought I was losing weight. *Yia yias* had been saying that to their children and grandchildren for generations. In the past, there were so many diseases (polio, rheumatoid fever, etc.) that decimated kids that the *yia yias* thought a kid who looked well fed was a healthy kid. And so, *yia yias* would load you up. You could have four helpings, but when you discreetly took your plate up to the sink, you'd hear, "*Then tha fas ahlow?*" (Aren't you going to eat more?) Then your *yia yia* would give you a look of utter devastation … and you'd go back and fill up one more helping.

I reassured *Yia Yia* that I wasn't losing weight and put an extra comforter over her to keep her warm. "Hey, if you come downstairs, remember not to say anything about the Greek guy I'm setting Angie up with. It's a surprise."

"No, I'll be staying up here. My legs and back are sore. I'm probably going to go to sleep soon." I was surprised she didn't want to meet the Greek guy, but she did look tired.

I left her room, went into the kitchen, and saw my mom by the oven. I saw the back of Angie's head as she watched television. I whispered quietly to my mom.

"Hey mom, Sophia's coming by with her friend Jerome to pick out the flowers for the wedding."

"Yeah, I talked to her today. She told me you decided to go to San Francisco for part of your honeymoon."

"Yeah, we'll be there for a week before we go to Greece." Mom seemed excited to talk about San Francisco because that's where she took her honeymoon, but I needed to talk to her about setting Angie up.

I motioned her over so that I could talk quietly to her, and Angie wouldn't hear me. She got my cue and came over to the corner of the kitchen. I looked back towards Angie who still had her head turned, watching television. "Now, Mom, you know some of the guys are meeting here tonight to do some work, right?"

"Right," she said.

"Listen, one of the guys who are helping us on this case is a Greek guy."

"Oh, wonderful." I motioned out to the living room couch where Angie was sitting watching television with her back to us.

"You know I'm thinking … maybe she meets him … something happens, who knows? But, do me a favor, don't say anything to anyone. Let it just happen. If Angie finds out, she'll leave."

"I won't. I promise. But Angie has no idea," my mom said.

"I know. That's good," I said.

"Hey, could one of you bring me my glass of soda that I left on the counter?" Angie called out from the den.

"Sure," I said. As I grabbed the glass, my mom looked out at Angie, worried. C'mon, this is the big set up, I was thinking. Why all the hesitation? I went into the living room and went to hand Angie the glass.

"Here, Ange …" I said as I handed her the glass. As Angie turned to get the glass, I saw that she had an ugly green facial mask and pedicure going and was dressed in some god awful, raggedy sweats.

"Oh, my God. What are you doing?" I asked her politely.

Okay, I yelled it.

She looked at me like I was nuts. "Shut up, I'm watching TV."

I picked up some Kleenex and tried to start wiping the mask off. The thing was painted onto her face. "Get that stuff off. Some of the guys from the office are coming by tonight."

"You didn't tell me anything."

"Yeah, yeah. Go upstairs and put on a nice dress … and some heels … and some perfume."

I think the heels and perfume requests may have been a bit much. Angie started to catch on. "Okay, what is your problem? Who's coming over, Michael?"

"I'm working here, okay? You're going to embarrass me." That was the best I could come up with.

"Fine. Whatever," she said in a huff.

Angie walked out of the kitchen and no sooner had the door swung closed when it swung back open to reveal *Yia Yia* dressed up and fresh as a spring chicken. This looked nothing like the *Yia Yia* I left minutes ago.

"*Yia Yia*, I thought you weren't feeling good?"

"I feel pretty good now. Thank the God." She made the sign of the cross and then leaned in to me. "Is the Greek boy here, yet?" she said conspiratorially.

"No, but I want to keep it quiet."

"Sure, sure," she said. Just then, Angie walked back in, still looking dreadful.

"I left my makeup bag down here." Suddenly, the doorbell rang. Everyone froze.

"Get behind the couch!" I yelled to Angie. But, it was too late, the door was already opening. In walked … Jerome, holding flowers. In perfect Greek, he said, "Hey everybody, how you doing?" *Yia Yia* stared at Jerome for a long moment and then turned to me, "He's Greek?"

Jerome, overhearing Yia Yia's question, yelled back in Greek, "Oh, yes, I am!" As *Yia*

Yia's jaw hit the ground in disbelief, Jerome saw Angie. "Love that mud mask," he exclaimed to her.

I explained to *Yia Yia* that Jerome was Sophia's friend, but I still don't think she got it. Just then, Sophia entered carrying some wedding flowers. She came over to me and gave me a kiss.

"Hi, honey. When Jerome and I finish the flowers, he said he'd help us with the first dance."

"Do you mind if we talk about that later," I said, stalling for time and not wanting to do the dreaded first dance. Angie was near the window and saw something outside.

"Hey, why are there a bunch of *yia yias* coming up our driveway?" said Angie.

"What?" I said. As Jerome, Angie and Sophia headed upstairs. I turned to the front door and saw a small army of *yia yias* coming in the house with food. I slowly turned to *Yia Yia*.

She read my face. "I didn't call anyone," she said innocently. After one more second of my staring, she broke. "Okay, I only called one," she said. "Voula. She's a big mouth that one." The *yia yias* marched in and started making themselves comfortable, asking where the Greek boy was. Just then, the kitchen door opened and Stan walked in.

"Oops, I guess I came in the wrong door."

All the *yia yias* went silent as they sized him up and down. I tried to distract from the obvious.

"Hi Stan, c'mon in …"

A moment later Todd and Mr. Witherspoon walked in, and I got us situated and working at one table as the *yia yias* started playing poker at another table. They were so obvious. They would play a little bit and then glance over and check out Stan. You could see each one of them sizing him up.

"Listen, tomorrow, we're going to be taking Mr. Witherspoon's old girlfriend's deposition," I said, trying not to pay attention to the *yia yias*. No sooner had I begun speaking when my *yia yia* came over carrying an oversized bowl of *avgolemono* soup and put it in front of Stan.

"A little *avgolemeno* soup for you."

"Oh … wow … thank you," said Stan. There was a pause as she waited for him to try it. A bit self-conscious, Stan finally did.

"Wow, that's just great," Stan said as he began to consume the soup.

"Oh, you like?" she said innocently. "Michael's sister, Angie, made it." *Yia Yia* smiled at him.

"You know *thee* Angie?"

"Um, no we haven't met," said Stan.

"She's a beautiful girl. Since she was a baby. Any boy who get to marry her, he is thee luckiest boy in the whole world." I gave *Yia Yia* a look trying to shoo her away.

"Angie is upstairs *Yia Yia*. I'm sure she'll be coming down soon," I said. I tried getting back to the legal stuff.

"Anyway, tomorrow, we'll be taking Mr. Witherspoon's former girlfriend's deposition, and a couple weeks after that, the trial will begin. So, Stan, I want you to be at her depo to get a feel for her."

"Sure," he said.

Yia Yia was still hovering like an airplane in a holding pattern, waiting for permission to land. Honest to God, she wasn't moving. You would have thought she was part of our legal team. I knew something was up. She smiled at Stan and then asked him in Greek, "Are you sick?" To the average observer this may have seemed to be a very innocuous question, but I knew exactly what *Yia Yia* was doing. She was testing his Greek. She was trying to see just how Greek he really was. Was he a Greek in name only? Or was he a *real* Greek who spoke the language fluently, celebrated Greek Independence Day, and had been back to visit his parents' *horio* (village) in Greece multiple times? Well, fortunately Stan spoke flawless Greek. He told her in Greek that he had a chest cold for the last couple days and couldn't get rid of it. *Yia Yia* studied him for a moment. Then she spoke up.

"Maybe you should try … a *venduza*."

I just about fell out of my chair. My *yia yia* and every *yia yia* I ever met believed that no matter what was ailing you, you could get rid of it by doing one of two things: a *venduza* or an *eglizma*. A *venduza* is an old school, homemade, Greek cure for I don't know what. It consists of pouring alcohol (sometimes just Ouzo) into a small glass, lighting it on fire like a blowtorch, distinguishing the fire, and then suctioning the hot glass right onto your ailing body part. It leaves a black mark on your body like you just walked out of a three-alarm fire. The heat was supposed to heal the ailing area. What the *yia yias* couldn't quite grasp was that America already had something that worked just as well: Bengay. For some reason Bengay wasn't good enough for them. I can't confirm this, but I swear that having the word gay in the label dissuaded them from ever trying the product. I could just see them warning a family member, "I no think so. You never know what could-a happen if a you put-a that on your body." So we were still relegated to *venduzas*.

Before I could move, the *yia yias* had jumped out of their chairs and mobilized. One got the alcohol, one got the glass, and another got the matches. They pulled Stan's shirt back and kaboom the *venduza* ignited higher than a flaming plate of *saganaki* (flaming cheese) They put the glass on his back and a moment later the *yia yias* finally took the suctioning glass off of Stan. He moved his arms around, coughed a little.

"I think I feel a little better," he said. All the *yia yias* smiled as he buttoned his shirt back up. Then they went back to their poker table to resume their game, proud of their accomplishment. Just then, Angie started coming down the stairs, dressed up and looking great. My mom was bringing out a tray of drinks. They arrived at the table at the same time. As my mom put down the drinks, she wiped her hands on a napkin to shake hands with Todd, whom she hadn't seen yet. Stan looked up and saw Angie. He stood up to greet her.

"Hi, I'm Stan. Great soup." A quizzical look came over Angie's face as she extended her hand. Just then, my mom extended her hand to say hello to Todd whom she'd just seen. As they went to say hello to each other and shake hands, all four of their hands crossed. Like line judges at Wimbledon, all of the *yia yias'* eyes shot over to watch the action. One *yia yia* whispered to another in Greek, "They're getting married."

The other one confirmed, "Oh, yeah."

It sounded crazy, but as I watched Angie and Stan continue to talk, I thought they did look compatible.

A few hours later, I escorted Mr. Witherspoon to the door. He showed a picture of his son to my Mom.

"Oh, how adorable," my mom said as she studied the picture. I walked up behind them.

"What are you looking at?"

"Your client's son," said my mom. Mr. Witherspoon showed me his kid's new grade school picture. I didn't mean to be rude, but I just didn't want to look. You get close to your clients, and you lose objectivity. Even more than that, it makes losing devastating. You not only let yourself down but your client, his family, and everyone else you've grown close to during the trial. It stays with you for years. I had learned to keep the emotional stuff out of it.

"Your kid will be on the stand for us. That's the only picture I need. I'll talk to you tomorrow."

Todd took Mr. Witherspoon out to his car, and I closed the door behind them. I came back inside and saw Stan entertaining the *yia yias* with one of his comedy bits before he headed for the door. He made them and Angie laugh—not an easy thing to do.

"It's open mike at the Improv next Wednesday, *Yia Yia*. I expect to see you there," he said.

The *yia yias* were like a bunch of groupies, cooing at the funny Greek boy.

"We'll be there," they said in unison. Stan headed for the door. Just then, I heard something and looked over to the *yia yias* who were gesturing wildly to me. Stan was headed for the wrong door. He'd come in from the back and was going out the front door. My life flashed in front of me. I went from zero to sixty in one second and got to the door before Stan did. He'd have to get over my dead body before I'd let him through that door.

"What are you trying to do, get me killed?" I asked Stan. I then led him towards the kitchen door where he'd entered. We exited the right way, and as I looked back, I saw *Yia Yia* smile at me.

Chapter Twenty

It was deposition day for Mr. Wither-spoon's ex-girlfriend, Maxine Smuthers. You have to be on your game during depositions. This is where you lay all the groundwork for the case and catch the other side lying. We held the deposition for Maxine in Surhoff's conference room. Surhoff kept us waiting for nearly thirty minutes, even though his client was already there. He would do any-thing just to throw you off your game.

Finally, Surhoff and Maxine entered the room, and I introduced them to Todd and Stan. When Surhoff introduced me to his client, he couldn't help but refer to me as "Mr. Alexis" again. As we were about to get started, I had Stan sit on an angle, a few seats away so he could get a feel for Maxine. This would help us when it came time to pick a jury. Surhoff looked angered that he was there, as if this was beneath him. He called in several lawyers who sat on his side of the table. Typical Surhoff, I thought. He did this to try and intimidate us. I began the deposition and got all the basic questions out of the way. Within a few minutes I was getting into the core of what I needed to know.

"… and do you recall how many times Mr. Witherspoon visited your son over the past three years."

"Infrequently," she said.

"But, you acknowledge that he has in fact visited with your son over the years." She started to hesitate. That's always the first sign that you've hit a flaw in their case. As she squirmed a bit, I noticed something in the reflection of the large glass wall beside them. There was a movement going on underneath their side of the table.

"I'm not acknowledging anything," she said defiantly. I leaned back and whispered to Todd to take the next question. I wanted to stare at the reflection this time. Todd jumped right in.

"Alright, let's break this down, then. In the last year, how many times did he visit your son?" asked Todd.

"Too few for me to remember," she said.

I didn't notice anything in the reflection this time. Maybe someone had just crossed their legs, I thought.

"More than ten visits?" Todd asked.

"Um ..." she said, again hesitating. She looked up trying to recall. As she did, I glanced over at the glass partition. I saw Surhoff tap her foot, indicating to her how to answer the question. She then answered.

"I don't remember," she said.

"Less than a hundred visits would you say?" asked Todd. Again, she hesitated, looking up, and Surhoff tapped her foot.

"Yes," she said. I had seen enough.

"Excuse me," I said turning to Maxine. "Just, so we are clear on this, when you are asked a question by counsel, your attorneys are not in any way allowed to indicate to you how to answer that question. Do you understand that?" Surhoff, who was leaning back in his chair, suddenly shot forward. "She fully understands that, Mr. Alexis, and I'm going to ask you to direct any further comments to me and—" I leaned towards Surhoff and cut him off. "I'll get to you in a second." Surhoff turned to the stenographer.

"Off the record!" he shouted. The stenographer immediately stopped typing. "Who do you think you're talking to?" Surhoff hissed at me. We were eye-to-eye across the table and the room went silent. I wasn't backing down. Enough was enough.

"If I see you tap your client's foot one more time to indicate to her how you want the question answered, you and I are going to have a problem,"

"Listen, Mr. Alexis, you watch—"

I rose out of my chair and let him have it. "It's Alexopoulos! Alexopoulos! And don't you ever call me anything but that again! Do you understand me?" I grabbed my brief-case and threw open the conference room door, causing all the glass windows to shake. "If there's anybody in this stinking law firm who does not understand that my name is Michael Alexopoulos, step over here and tell me what you think my name is!"

The entire floor was silent. One or two heads peeked up to see what had happened. No one said a word. "Good! We got that clear!" I looked back at Surhoff. I had enough of him, his antics, and his law firm's bullying. "You wanna play rough with me? You wanna make this ugly? Then, you go get all your five-hundred dollar an hour goons and let's have at it."

I was about to leave, but had to get one last punch in. "You know, all of you think you are so smart, with your fancy Ivy League degrees. Let me tell you something they never taught you at those schools." I looked around the room at the whole of them. "Don't piss off a Greek."

I walked out of the room with Todd right behind me. Stan, still in shock by the outburst took a few moments to gather up his stuff. As he did, an attorney leaned over to Surhoff.

"I didn't know Tigers could grow back their teeth." He got up and exited, leaving Surhoff alone. A moment later, Stan who had finally gathered up his stuff, made his way over to Surhoff and nervously handed him his card.

"I guess we'll need to re-schedule this. Just give me a call if you need to coordinate times and dates." As Stan headed out, Surhoff looked at the card. "Stan the comedian. Chuckles are my business," Surhoff said reading Stan's card.

"Oops, wrong card," Stan said as he quickly pulled a card from his other pocket and gave it to Surhoff.

As Todd and I got into the elevator, the nervous energy of the explosion was still with us, but neither of us spoke. Finally, as we descended, Todd looked over to me. "Seriously … I think that was the best thirty seconds I've ever had practicing law," he said, breaking the silence. "And I want to say one thing to you—if I have ever even slightly mispronounced your last name, I completely and totally apologize."

That got me to laugh. As we got off the elevator, we both knew that Surhoff's law firm had the fire power to wipe us out in this case, but so be it. I wasn't going quietly into that gentle night.

Chapter Twenty-one

Home movies of my family played in the darkened living room of my apartment. I sat there alone watching all the videos we had taken as a family as we celebrated life together. It was the last piece of property I had to divide up between my parents. Some footage of me dancing when I was eight years old came on the screen. All around the room I danced, waving a napkin in the air: innocent; unscarred; full of hope, love, and laughter.

More footage of my family appeared. This time Angie was in it, clowning around with me at Christmas time. Then some footage of my parents: My mom showed off her new Christmas clothes. My parents shared a kiss. There was innocence about all of us, as though none of us could have ever known what was coming.

"Knock, knock."

I looked back across the room and saw Sophia standing in the doorway.

"How's it going?" she asked.

"I've got everything divided up between them. I just have to figure out who gets these," I said as I gestured to the boxes of photos and videos.

Those boxes held the stories of our lives. I felt as though I should take those memories out to a field and bury them with the date our family began and the date it ended like the remains of a person who had passed away.

Sophia sat next to me and together we watched my family saying a prayer before Easter dinner. Everyone's head was bowed.

"Great family, huh?" I said.

"Yeah."

"I'm going to miss it."

"They'll still be around."

"It'll never be the same again. We'll never sit around a dinner table together again. Never just hang out and watch TV together.

Holidays, church, birthdays—we'll never be together again. We're not a family anymore."

The video clip ended, and I put in another tape. A moment later, footage from my parents' wedding started to play. "How are you supposed to say goodbye to all of this? I mean, it's just … over."

On screen, my parents shared a kiss. They were so young and in love. "Look at them," I said.

My parents kissed again and mugged for the camera. Nothing but blue skies in front of them. "What went wrong?"

"A lot of things, I bet," said Sophia.

What really does cause a marriage to crumble, I wondered? Do couples know on their wedding day that it is not going to work? Or do they all start out like Sophia and me and think they're going to make it? Does one incident start the downfall of a marriage? Or do small incidents accumulate over the years and wear down the love two people have for one another? Do time, taxes, bills, ageing, and the hardships of life simply make it too hard for people to remember the love they once had for each another?

I put in another video and pressed play. A few moments went by, and then I saw myself and Sophia as teenagers in our backyard. Sophia laughed, and so did I.

"Hey, that's us. What's this from?" she asked.

I looked down at the video box, read it. "Our graduation party from junior high. My dad must have taken some videos that day." Both of us were laughing and smiling, eating cake. As we clowned around, the camera slowly moved off of us, over to the nearby tree house. We could see the carving Sophia had made so many years earlier.

"Sophia and Michael ... forever."

As Sophia and I sat on the couch quietly watching the videos, we held hands. The video of us ended with young Sophia and I exchanging a kiss.

Our thoughts were interrupted by the ringing phone. Sophia answered it and cupped the phone.

"It's *Yia Yia*. She wants you to know she found a secretary for you."

"Tell her, I'll take whoever it is. The ones Todd hired have been awful." Sophia listened for a moment. "Oh, and she's from a Greek family. Well, she's a shoe in then."

I laughed and told Sophia to have the girl fax over her resume, and that Todd and I would meet with her. I whispered to Sophia that *Yia Yia* was probably calling because she needed a ride somewhere. Sophia went back to the phone and told *Yia Yia* to have the girl fax her resume over, and then she asked her if she needed a ride anywhere tonight. Sophia listened for a moment.

"Oh, Stan's performing tonight. It is open mike at the Laugh-In Comedy Shop." Sophia looked over at me, and I nodded to her. "Okay, we'll come pick you up," she told *Yia Yia*.

The Laugh-In Comedy Shop was packed. All the *yia yias* were there, decked out in traditional *yia yia* black. I'm not sure they'd ever been to one of these before. As I walked up to the door, *Yia Yia* Penelope held me back for a moment. I thought she was going to say thanks for giving her a ride over.

But, she had something else on her mind. In Greek, she let me know what it was.

"What's this I hear you don't want to do a special first dance for Sophia at your wedding?"

Oh, great, busted. I didn't realize *Yia Yia* and Sophia were becoming such great friends.

"C'mon *Yia Yia*, it's just a first dance," I said. *Yia Yia* wasn't buying that.

"Hey, listen mister. She's trying to make you happy, you better try and make her happy, too. Understand? Remember ... the door swings both ways."

Jerome just happened to walk by and heard *Yia Yia*. "Oh-oh, somebody got *Yia Yia* mad," he said in Greek as he walked by.

I rolled my eyes and finally headed in.

Stan was awesome. He made all of us laugh hard. I don't think there was a person who didn't get skewered in his act. At one point, Stan asked to have the house lights turned up.

"Let's see who is out there tonight," he said. He walked over to our table and leaned over the edge of the stage. "This is my friend,

Michael Alexopoulos. He's getting married … and this must be your fiancé. Either that, or you have a lot of explaining to do, Michael."

The audience laughed and he turned to Sophia. "What's your name?"

"Sophia Graff," said Sophia. Stan mused over her last name." Graff," he said musingly.

We all started laughing, knowing what he was about to say. "Now, that's an interesting Greek name. Let me ask you … what part of Greece does the Graff family come from, Sophia?"

Everyone started howling as she leaned into the mike and let everyone know she wasn't Greek. "Oh, you're not Greek!" he proclaimed, as he put his arm around her and whispered. "Get out while you can. Don't you realize what you're getting into?"

"Well, I'm learning," said Sophia.

"Really? So what have you learned so far?"

"Well … whatever illness anyone in my family has from now on, I'll blame it on the evil eye." The audience started laughing and she continued, "I need to buy a set of worry beads the size of a garden hose and an equally large Bible, put them on our living room table and never touch them." The audience was cracking up. "And although the wedding day is said to be the official day we get married, it really won't be official until we honeymoon in Greece, and I get a picture taken of me riding on a donkey in my in-laws *horio*." The audience was roaring.

"Hey, wait let me get a pen, this is good stuff," said Stan.

"And the moment we get married ... I pledge to hate every Turk that ever lived," said Sophia. The audience broke out into huge laughter and applause led by *Yia Yia* Penelope. Sophia took a bow. She was just awesome.

I had to do my part. I leaned over to Jerome and said, "Any girl who can put up with all of us, I've gotta do a first dance for."

"So, you want me to choreograph a big first dance?" asked Jerome.

"Well, let's not go overboard here ..."

"I'll start on it tonight," he said.

"But, listen, you have to promise me that Sophia doesn't know anything. I really want this to be a surprise for her." Jerome did an imaginary buttoning of his lips and tossed away the key.

Over the next few months, I snuck away whenever I could to learn country dancing. The hardest part was not having my partner. So, Jerome made a life sized cutout of Sophia, and I danced across the floor of his spin class room, with it. I actually enjoyed thinking about how much it would mean to Sophia. I could see how hard she was trying. *Yia Yia* was teaching her how to cook Greek dishes, she was reading books about Greek culture, and Sophia actually got *Yia Yia* to get the computer out of the box and learn to use it. That was a miracle in and of itself. Life was definitely looking up.

Chapter Twenty-two

One day, the yia yia mafia came to Sophia's apartment to have a little talk. They settled in around the kitchen table. Sophia sat at one end and, surrounded by all of yia yias who looked angry. "There's a little problem, Sophia," said Yia Yia Penelope. Sophia hesitated, sensing they were upset.

"Something I'm doing wrong?" All of the *yia yias* nodded. "What is it?"

"Sophia, you show up on time for everything. You're never late," said *Yia Yia*.

"That's bad?"

"Horrible," the *yia yias* said in unison. *Yia Yia* took a deep breath. "We need to teach you about Greek time."

"Greek time? What is Greek time?" asked Sophia.

"Say a party begins at 7:00 PM. What time do you think the most important person will arrive at the party? Probably about 8:00 PM," said *Yia Yia* answering her own question. "So, you show up fifteen minutes after that person."

"Now, you are thee most important person at the party," chimed in another *yia yia*.

"That's-a Greek time," said another *yia yia*.

"Okay," said Sophia kind of understanding it all.

"In general, start being late," said *Yia Yia*. All the other *yia yias* nodded in agreement. "Dinners, parties, birthdays, baptisms … just start showing up late."

"But what do I say when they ask me why I'm late?"

"Greek time," in unison said all the *yia yias*.

"Okay, I think I've got it."

"And by the way, the dress you are wearing is beautiful," said *Yia Yia* Penelope.

"Thank you," said Sophia. An instant later, she realized it was a test, and she quickly spit three times.

"The *pastitsio* you made the other day was perfect. Can I have the recipe?" asked another *yia yia*.

"Sure," said Sophia. She looked around the kitchen and pulled out a recipe and handed it to the *yia yia*.

"There you go. That's the one that I kept two ingredients out of."

"Good," responded the *yia yia*. "Now, you're learning." All the *yia yias* smiled. Sophia felt like she was on a roll.

"Okay, now, can you explain one other thing to me?"

"Sure," said *Yia Yia*.

"How do you do that special Greek wave?"

"The Greek wave?" said *Yia Yia*. All the *yia yias* looked at each other quizzically.

"Yeah, I noticed whenever you are talking to each other and you get real excited, you wave at each other like this ..." said Sophia.

Sophia held up her right hand and did what kind of looked like an American high five to the group of the *yia yias*. The *yia yias'* eyes went wide open. Sophia didn't realize this was the Greek equivalent to flipping someone off.

"Hey, I guess, I've got it down pretty good," said Sophia. She then turned to the *yia yias* on the other side of the table, laid one on them to more horrified looks. "*Opa!*" shouted Sophia as she did it again. She did it to another group of *yia yias*. One of the *yia yias* gave Sophia a "Greek wave" back.

"Hey, back at ya," an exuberant Sophia shouted as she did it again. *Yia Yia* Penelope jumped up and quickly escorted Sophia out of the room. "Okay, we need to talk about this," said *Yia Yia* quietly.

"Did I do something wrong?"

"You just cursed everyone in the room."

Chapter Twenty-three

There were arrows, cross outs, and scribbles everywhere on our wedding seating chart. As I concentrated on the chart, which we'd put in the corner of my apartment, I heard Sophia get off the phone.

"Well, what did they say?" I asked.

"Nope. None of them can make it. They're going to be out of the country," she said with disappointment. She plopped down on the couch near me. "That's fifteen of my relatives who can't make it. And I still don't know who to ask to walk me down the aisle." I sat next to her on the couch and tried to assure her that we'd figure everything out.

"I wanna go home. I miss everyone," she said quietly.

"I bet I can make you feel better."

"No you can't."

I went over to a piano in the corner of the room. "Come here."

Sophia made her way over to the piano, sulking the whole way, and finally plunked down next to me. I began to play the first few notes of "Rocky Top:" the official state song of Tennessee. This was the song Sophia played so many years ago when we danced beneath the tree house as youngsters. As I slowly played the chords of the song, I began to sing. It wasn't quite in tune, but I got the words right.

"Wish I was on ol' Rocky Top, down in the Tennessee hills. Ain't no smoggy smoke on Rocky Top; ain't no telephone bills ..." Sophia began to smile. "Rocky Top, you'll always be home sweet home to me. Good ol' Rocky Top, Rocky Top, Tennessee, Rocky Top, Tennessee." I stopped singing for a moment. "Another verse?" She smiled and nodded, and I started another verse.

"Once I had a girl on Rocky Top, half bear, other half cat, wild as a mink, sweet as soda pop. I still dream about that." Sophia moved closer and sang the chorus with me.

"Rocky Top, you'll always be home sweet home to me. Good ol' Rocky Top, Rocky Top, Tennessee, Rocky Top Tennessee …"

As we finished singing the song, Sophia gave me a kiss and looked at me. It reminded me of that night so many years ago. She still had a way of making me feel like I was the most important person in the world.

"I know two more verses," I said, bragging a bit.

"Save 'em for later." She pulled me off the bench onto the floor and gave me another kiss.

Chapter Twenty-four

Believe it or not, I talked everyone into cowboy dancing with Jerome, and they agreed to keep it a secret. Stan and Angie showed up and so did a bunch of the yia yias. Once a week, we'd sneak away, and Jerome would stand in the middle of the floor where he taught spin classes and shout out instructions with a megaphone. I was actually starting to get the hang of it. I kept thinking about Sophia's reaction and how happy it would make her.

We were wrapping up our practice session for the night. Angie, Stan, the *yia yias,* and I were all getting something to drink before we called it a night. I could see the *yia yias* in the corner talking about how great Stan and Angie looked together. I could hardly believe how well they got along.

Just then, Jerome came over. "What do you think? Am I starting to get the hang of it?" I asked him.

"Sophia is going to love it. But I've got to add one little touch to it," he said. Jerome reached into a bag he'd brought and pulled out a cowboy hat.

"There you go, 'pardner. Next week, we'll do a little Cotton-Eyed Joe."

I tried it on, and all the *yia yias*, Stan, and Angie checked it out in the mirror. We all took turns trying it on, and had a good laugh when *Yia Yia* tried it on.

As we were looking in the mirror, I looked over at a security monitor that taped outside the studio and saw Sophia coming up the steps. Everybody screamed and scattered. We ran like mice and hid under mats, in closets, behind the sound system, wherever we could find a place.

A moment later, Sophia walked up to the glass entrance doors and waved animatedly as she saw Jerome. I've never seen Jerome speechless. He just stood there like a pole as though she couldn't see him.

"Oh, great you're here!" Sophia said as she entered. She ran up to Jerome and gave him a big hug.

"Hey, what's going on?" Jerome said, finally speaking.

"What are you doing here alone?"

"Um, I'm working on some new spin routines."

"Oh, I'm sorry I didn't call."

"No problem," Jerome said as he changed subjects, "So, did you need something?"

I looked over and saw *Yia Yia's* black shawl hanging on a spin bicycle right next to where Sophia was sitting. I was trying to motion to Jerome but he didn't look over at me. I glanced over at *Yia Yia* underneath the mats. She motioned to me to be quiet, as though that thought hadn't already crossed my mind.

"Well, I hate to ask you this in a rush," said Sophia, "But … you know I don't have anyone to walk me down the aisle on my wedding day. I always wanted this to be the most special walk of my life, and I couldn't think of anyone more special than you to share it with. So, I came by to ask you if you would walk me down the aisle."

"Me? You want me to walk you down the isle?" Jerome said as he started to get choked up. Sophia nodded and smiled. There was no one more deserving. He was the one who had been there for Sophia during the tough times.

"I would be honored. It means so much to me that you thought of me," Jerome said.

"Michael was the one who suggested it. And everyone, *Yia Yia*, Angie, our parents agreed you were the perfect choice."

"Okay, now I'm going to cry." Jerome said as he reached for what he thought was a towel, but was my *yia yia's* shawl. He quickly dabbed his eyes with it and tossed in a near-by bin, realizing what it was.

"Well, I'll let you get back to your routines," said Sophia. "You're the greatest, Jerome," she said as she exited. After Sophia had cleared the building, everyone raced out of their hiding places and ran up to Jerome whooping and hollering happily. He sat there in the middle of all his friends and took in the joyful moment.

Chapter Twenty-five

As my sister Angie and I entered the courtroom, a placard on the door read, "Alexopoulos vs. Alexopoulos". She and I both paused and looked at it for a moment. We never thought we'd see that. We made our way to some seats and watched Judge Samuels enter from his chambers after his lunch break. He discarded a food wrapper under his desk, and the clerk handed him some papers. He stared at them for a few seconds and then looked up at my mom and dad who stood before him. "Have both parties agreed to the settlement as set forth before me?

"I have," said my mother.

"I have," said my dad.

"Alright then, the court accepts this mutually agreed upon settlement and stipulates that Georgia Alexopoulos and Harry

Alexopoulos are by their mutual agreement officially divorced in accordance with the laws of the State of Illinois."

He thumped his gavel and that was it. He turned to his assistant. "What do we have next?"

It was so cold, so emotionless. Over forty years of marriage, and with one thump of the gavel, it was over. When someone dies, at least they have a funeral, I thought. Angie and I watched our parents begin to go their separate ways.

"Who do we follow out?" she asked.

"Go with mom. I think I may have to give dad a lift home. I smelled some alcohol on his breath during the break," I said.

I ended up giving my dad a lift home and Angie gave my mom a ride. It turned out both of them had been drinking. The alcohol made them both speak freely.

"How in the world did we end up here?" my dad said out loud as he stared out the window of my car.

"Ah, who am I kidding? It's simple … In the beginning, everything works. You come home, she rubs your back, makes you dinner, tells you you're the greatest …" He let out a sigh, as his mind seemed to sift back in time.

"But then the years go by, kids come along, she doesn't go to the ball games with you anymore. She doesn't want to hear your problems anymore. All she's concerned about is whether you put money in the bank, because the mortgage is due. Take the garbage out, paint this, fix that … and by the way, I'd really like those diamond earrings for Christmas. You realize, you're working harder than you ever have, but where is the love? She's not giving it to you. Your kids aren't giving it to you—they've got their own things to do. But, where's the love?"

As Angie drove along, she got the reverse story from my mom. "Weekends he was working. Holidays he was working. Vacations! He was working. And you know what? That became his family. He got so wound into that lifestyle, he couldn't get out of it. All his highs and lows came from his work."

As I turned down another side street, my Dad continued to speak. "… and then one day, you look in the mirror and you say,

'Who in the world is that old guy?' and you start thinking 'How many good years do I have left?' I mean good, healthy years. No pills. No walkers. How many? Ten? Fifteen? Twenty? And you think to yourself … are they all going to be like this? Just being a money machine, making everyone else's life happy?"

Angie pulled up to some railroad tracks and waited for the train to pass by. My mom barely noticed as she continued her thoughts out loud, "You start to feel like a maid. You clean up the house. You cook the food. You wash the dishes. Finally, you look around and say, 'Hey, where's my husband? Aren't we supposed to be enjoying our life together? Isn't there some fun in all this?'"

My Dad looked over at me for a moment and then looked back out the window. "Try living without love or affection. It gets to you after awhile. You try to do it because of the kids and all that, but it gets lonely … and right about that time, you're in a bank, a grocery store, or eating alone in some restaurant … and all it takes is a sneeze, a dropped napkin, or a spilled drink … and some woman gives you a smile. On any other day, you would have smiled and looked away, but not that day. On that day, you let your smile linger for just a moment longer, and in that moment, you know and she knows that you just opened the door. And then someone new comes into your life."

My father's eyes softened with sadness. "All because you just wanted a little love and affection."

My mother searched through her purse looking for tissue as Angie pulled up to her driveway. "I just wanted someone to share my life with. Enough was enough. I couldn't take it anymore. So, I looked elsewhere."

My father finally closed his eyes and exhaled. "That's how it happens."

So, that was it. My parents were officially divorced. When I talked to my sister Angie later, I realized that my parents had probably never told each other what they told us that day. Had they talked, I think they would have realized that they both wanted the same thing. You see, I don't think either of them ever really knew what mattered to the other person.

I think each partner has to know what is sacred to the other in a marriage. Is it money, culture, children, sex, career? What do we hold so sacred that we would be willing to walk away from our spouse if we didn't have it in our marriage?

Unfortunately for my parents, I don't think they ever talked to each other about what they held to be sacred in their marriage.

What I learned at Church Camp – Lesson #6

"It's sacred. That's why it's a sacrament."

Every morning at the camp, we would go to church services to celebrate the Divine Liturgy and take communion. To a young kid who had spent a large portion of the night before talking to other campers, celebrate wasn't exactly the word that came to mind as I was roused out of bed and went to the church hall to participate in the Divine Liturgy.

Once the liturgy started, I always thought about how much I appreciated our choir at home that we always complained about because at camp, we were the choir. After every petition the priest cued us, and the campers would groggily sing back, "*kyrie eleison*" or "amen".

As the service went on, I thought about all the events that were going to take place that day and tried to sing, "amen" just a little faster so we could start the day.

Finally, the priest came out with the communion chalice and said, "With fear of God, with faith, and with love draw near." This signaled to me that the service was just about over.

On this particular day, everybody was taking communion, and I was in the back so I was last in line. With only one priest serving communion, the line moved along slowly. Finally, there was only one camper in front of me. He said his name, took communion, and then it was my turn. However, just as the camper turned away, he lifted his arm to make the sign of the cross and inadvertently hit the chalice. The priest was able to stop the chalice from falling, but in the process the contents spilled out onto the floor.

Every one of us gasped. It was awful seeing everything spill, but there was nothing any of us could do to stop it. Several of us started to move towards the priest to help him, but he held his hand up, signifying for us to stop. He put the chalice down, got on his knees, and with his mouth and hands he consumed every speck of the communion that had fallen.

There was nothing left on the floor when he stood up. It was spotless. Nonetheless, he went over and got some towels.

He took the towels and wiped the floor repeatedly, looking from every angle to see if he had missed anything. Finally, he stood up, called over an assistant, and proceeded to burn the towels.

It was only then that he addressed us. In a calm voice he said, "What happened was an accident. But it's important to remember that we believe that the body and blood of Christ are in that chalice. It's sacred. That's why we call it a sacrament."

He then looked at me. I was the only person left, and he said, "Michael, I'm sorry, there is no more communion. You'll have to wait until tomorrow." I nodded and headed back to my seat. The camper who knocked the chalice apologized to me, but I told him not to worry about it.

It was strange, I felt empty inside. The feeling stayed with me the whole day. What I had taken for granted moments earlier suddenly meant more to me than I'd realized. The next day, I was the first in line for communion. As the priest addressed me and said, "The servant of God," and I said my name in Greek, I felt myself get choked up. I never looked at communion the same after that.

Lesson learned: God is sacred.

Chapter Twenty-six

It was Friday night and Greektown was bustling. Every restaurant seemed to be overflowing. On any other night, I would have loved this but not on the night of my parents' divorce. I knew within minutes I'd have a friend coming up, wanting to talk about it. To the average person, that probably doesn't sound reasonable. The divorce just became final that afternoon. How could anyone know about it? But, to us Greeks, a couple hours is a lifetime to spread the word. You see, there is only one thing we love to see more than a Greek who succeeds—a Greek who fails. And the news travels at warp speed. When we were kids, we used to say that if you want people to know something there were three ways to get the word out quickly: tele-phone, tele-fax, and tele-Greek.

I had told Sophia I was going to meet her at the Mykonos restaurant, but I didn't feel like seeing anyone at that moment. I called her on my cell phone.

"It's over. They can both go their own ways, do their own thing." Sophia could hear the mood I was in, so she just listened. "Let's just forget about tonight. It's an hour wait. I'm not going to sit around for an hour just to eat some stupid Greek food," I said.

"Okay, I'm almost there. Just wait on the corner," she said. I thought seeing Sophia might help my mood, so I agreed to hang out and wait. I hung up the phone and waited off to the side of the restaurant, near an alleyway. As I stood there, I heard some music coming from down the alley. I looked down and saw the guys in the band that were going to be playing at our wedding. They were taking a break from playing in the restaurant.

Costas, the lead singer, spotted me as I peeked down the alley. "Hey, Michael. I heard we're playing at your wedding!" he yelled when he saw me. He held up a drink. "Get over here. Let's toast."

I walked over, and he poured me some wine. "So, what's this I hear you've got a bluegrass band playing at your wedding?" I laughed and smiled. "There's an old saying …" he said. "At every funeral, there is a laugh and at every wedding there is a tear." We clinked glasses and drank. After a moment, he continued, "Sorry to hear about your parents."

"Oh, you heard," I said.

"It's on the *yia yia* hot wire …"

What did I tell you? I'd known Costas for years, and I knew he didn't mean anything by it. He wasn't the type who would ask for details. So, I felt comfortable around him and the other band members.

"Are you eating inside?"

"It's an hour wait," I said. He pounded on a nearby window. It opened a second later, and he yelled at one of the waiters, pointing to me. The employee hollered back and slammed the window.

"Five minutes," said Costas. He picked up his *bouzouki*, strummed it a little bit. "It's better out here, anyway. We've got wine, a little cheese, some bread, the music, the stars … what more do you need?" He started strumming a little more on his *bouzouki*. "C'mon, I'll play a song for you? We'll both feel better."

I told him I was too beaten up from the day to dance, but Costas started playing anyway. As he started strumming his *bouzouki*, the other musicians picked up their instruments and began to slowly join in.

"You have to dance, otherwise the devil wins. He brings all this bad news to you and loves to see you walk out of here like you are." Costas imitated my worn out posture: head down, shoulders slouched. He smiled and said, "That's why God invented the *bouzouki*. So we could dance and forget life's problems for a little while."

After a few moments, I got up. As the bittersweet song played, the music slowly seeped into the night. I took my coat off and started dancing in the alley.

As the music echoed off the brick walls, it felt good to be free from the pain I felt for a few minutes. But Costas was not going to let me enjoy the slow stuff too much, and after a few moments, he began to pick up the tempo of the music. I began dancing quicker, going around the table and under the awning. As the beat got even faster, I picked up a napkin and jumped on the table where Costas was playing. I whipped the napkin above my head as I danced. Down at the end of the alleyway, Jerome pulled up as he was dropping Sophia off at the restaurant. She got out of the car, looked down the alley, and realized it was me.

"Look at him, Jerome," she said. Jerome peered over the hood of the car and smiled. "I don't ever want to lose him."

"I keep telling you Ms. Sophia, he's not your daddy. He's a whole different human being." She watched in the distance as I whipped the white napkin into the night, the music careening off the brick alleyway walls and finally coming to an end. I was exhausted, but I felt alive. Costas winked at me as he put his *bouzouki* away, "And the devil losses again".

A few minutes later, Sophia and I were seated in the main section of the restaurant. Sophia watched as I tried to figure out what I was going to order. She interrupted my thoughts. "Michael …" she said. At first I didn't look up because I thought she was just talking casually to me as we ordered. But, a moment later, she slid her hand across the table and cupped it into my hand and looked at me. I looked up. "This is it, right?" Her question cut through all the noise and din of the loud restaurant. "I mean, it's you and me, all the way to the end, no matter what, right?"

"Yeah, all the way to the end."

"I couldn't handle it if I lost you, Michael," she said softly.

"I'm not going anywhere, Sophia."

It's funny. Some people might wonder why she asked me that question at that moment. I knew exactly why. When Sophia saw me dancing in the alleyway, it affected her. It reinforced something she loved about me and this was her way of expressing her vulnerabilities about losing me. A waiter arrived at our table with some of the appetizers we had ordered. As he walked back towards the kitchen, Sophia picked up her napkin and began to unfold it but then held it in her hands and looked at me. "I wanna do this one day while I'm dancing," she said as she waved the napkin in the air as I had done.

The napkin, I thought, that's what she saw in the alley that made her emotional.

"What does that mean when you do that?" she asked. She waved the napkin again and looked over to me. I knew that for some reason this answer meant something to her, so I didn't want to give her fluff. I thought back to all the times either myself or some relative had waved a napkin while dancing, as I searched for the answer myself.

"When I was a kid, I used to get my parents together in our family room, and we'd push all the furniture to the side, and I'd run in the kitchen and grab a napkin off the table."

I took the napkin off my lap. "And they'd put on this *bouzouki* music … It would start real slow, but by the end of the song, the *bouzouki* would go real fast, and I'd be out there dancing. I didn't know any of the steps, but I'd jump around the room kicking my feet and whipping the napkin in the air."

Sophia smiled as I continued. "I was just a kid, but even then, there was something I understood about all of that—the dancing, the music, waving that napkin in the air—that's how we approached life …" I waved my napkin slightly. "It was like we were saying, whatever has happened, the good, the bad … I accept it. Because I'm here today, I'm alive, the music is playing, and I'm surrounded by people I love. I'm free."

Sophia's eyes welled up as I finished. I should have known. Freedom. That's what Sophia saw in the waiving napkin. I put the napkin back on the table. Sophia smiled at me and held up her glass of wine. In Greek, no less, she toasted us. "To us."

We clinked glasses, and I replied to her. "To us."

I've heard that when you get married, your joy is doubled and your sorrow is shared. It must be true, because on that day, just being with Sophia cut the sorrow I felt from my parents' divorce in half.

Chapter Twenty-seven

The trial finally began, and we were in the middle of jury selection. Trials are often won or lost on jury selection. After what happened at Surhoff's office, he wanted to crush me. He meticulously surveyed each juror, looking for any possible edge he could get.

"Your honor, we'd like to thank jurors #86 and #146 for coming today." The two potential jurors got up and left. I leaned over and talked to Stan. He had some great suggestions, but I was playing a hunch and was going to go with it.

"Mr. Alexopoulos?" said the judge.

"Your honor, we'd like to thank jurors #23 and juror #45 for coming today." These two jurors got up and left, leaving only women remaining on the jury. I knew having an all female jury was a gamble. As much as I disliked Surhoff, he could be charming, and that could be a problem with an all female jury. But I felt the females would be empathetic to the son when he took the stand. It felt like Surhoff and I were locked in a cerebral chess match. Just then, I heard my Dad's voice.

"Excuse me, your honor. Counsel would like a five minute recess." I couldn't believe he was there and had the audacity to interrupt.

"Mr. Alexopoulos, are you part of Mr. Witherspoon's legal team?" the judge asked.

"Yes," said my Dad.

"No," I said at the same moment.

What a mess. We quickly adjourned and our side made it into a conference room at the courthouse. My dad and I began to yell at each other across the table.

"What do you think you're doing?" I yelled at my Dad.

"What am I doing? What are you doing? You're putting all women on that jury! Are you crazy?" he shouted back.

"It's my case! It's my case! I don't need your advice!"

"Let me tell you, people pay me a lot of money for my advice! And I'm telling you a jury full of women is not going to win this case! What little chance you had of winning this case, just walked out the door!" At that moment, I'm surprised Mr. Witherspoon didn't have a heart attack as I spun his chair around and pointed to him.

"When his kid walks in here and testifies about missing his father, those women will sympathize with that kid," I said.

"You're acting like it's a done deal that the judge is going to let the kid testify!" said my dad.

"The court psychologist recommended that the kid testify!"

"You're in front of Judge Hinderland. He'll blow his nose with that recommendation!"

"No he won't! And when that kid gets up there and says 'I love my dad, I want to be with him' this case is over."

"Michael, I know you and—"

"No, you don't know me. You know who I am to you? I'm an old employee that you fired one day! That's it! You have no idea who I am!"

"I give up! You want to paint yourself in a corner, do it!" My Dad walked out, slamming the door, as I left through another door. Mr. Witherspoon stared on, stunned. He looked over at Stan.

"That's just how Greeks communicate," said Stan.

"My people are the same way. Yelling and screaming, but in the end we love each other." said Mr. Witherspoon.

We went back to the courtroom, and I committed to have an all female jury. Our case was going to rise or fall on that decision.

Chapter Twenty-eight

As I studied at my office desk, I kept thinking about my argument with my dad. Yes, I had taken a risk, but I thought it was a smart and calculated one. You don't beat the Surhoffs of the world with a bread and butter approach. You have to do something that throws them off their game. I leaned back in my chair and stretched for a moment. I glanced over at the old picture of Todd and me dancing, briefcases in hand, exuding a sheer naivety about life. A beat later, my thoughts were interrupted as Todd walked in. "Hey, we've got an interview for the secretary job.

"Who is it today?"

"The girl your *yia yia* sent over to us." We walked out towards the main office, just as the applicant was knocking at the door.

"I'll get it," I said. I opened the door, and saw *Yia Yia* standing with a resume in her hand. Next to her was Sophia. "What are you doing here?" I asked.

"I brought her by for her interview," said Sophia.

"Her interview?"

"I'm the Greek girl. I'm looking for a job," said *Yia Yia*. She walked in and handed me her resume.

"I'm great on the phone. I can type," she said and then added with a smile, "And I know how to use a computer." I looked over at Todd for his thoughts. He shrugged at me.

"Well ... what kind of wages are you looking for?" I said ribbing her.

Yia Yia pointed to Sophia. "She negotiates for me." Everyone laughed. Just then, the phone rang. All of us looked at the ringing phone for a moment.

"You're hired," I said as I pointed at the ringing phone. How much worse could *Yia Yia* be than the disasters we'd hired so far, I thought? She was reliable, honest and would show up on time. *Yia Yia* settled into the secretary chair, answered the phone like an old pro, and started getting everything organized.

Chapter Twenty-nine

Fr. Jim was closing up the church, as we conducted our last one-on-one marital session. He went around closing doors, turning off lights, and blowing out candles. He was so busy that we frequently had our sessions while he was doing other things. I didn't mind it because it didn't seem so formal.

"Tell me about that day you lost the Blue Steel case," he said. I hated talking about that day. It was one of the worst of my life. Gut wrenching.

"I remember waking up that morning and thinking 'this is a perfect day,'" I said.

"What was perfect about it?"

"Everything. I was working for one of the biggest law firms in the city. I had money. I was engaged to a Greek girl," I said. "My life was set. Everything was perfect."

"And then you lost the case?"

"Yeah."

"You said you lost the case in your clos-ing argument? What happened?" I explained to him that when you give a closing argu-ment, the jury wants to hear what's in your gut. They want to hear your voice. I was more concerned about whether my dad would like my closing argument. I was try-ing to remember everything that I knew he wanted me to say instead of summarizing in my own thoughts. But, there are no excuses. The bottom line was I gave a horrible clos-ing, and we lost.

"Then you showed up to the firm the next day, and your dad fired you?" I simply nodded. "That must have been tough," he said. "I'm sure you tried your hardest during the trial."

"My dad's favorite saying is: the client doesn't pay you to try hard; the client pays you to win." Fr. Jim had pretty much finished closing up the church, and we stood in the church's center, surrounded by the icons. "Bottom line, I didn't win. So, I was out. It's a business."

"You ever worry that all that anger you have inside of you could hurt your marriage?"

"What anger?" I said as I smiled.

"C'mon. Your dad fires you in front of the entire staff. No conversation. No notice. He just cuts you off. You have to start your own practice from scratch, no clients, no financial support. How many loans did you have to take out just to get on your feet?"

I didn't respond. He was right. It was a nightmare trying to get going again, and I wasn't going to deny it.

"You probably wanted to throw him off that building he worked in. And my guess is that this was a breaking point of a bad relationship."

"We never had a relationship. He never had time for one." Like I said, I didn't like reliving the past. What was the point? "Look, that's all old news," I said. "There's no point in talking about that stuff. Whatever my feelings are towards my dad, that doesn't have anything to do with my marrying Sophia."

"It has everything to do with it," said Fr. Jim. "There's no magic to this stuff, Michael.

Happy sons make loving husbands, and they become wonderful fathers." He took a moment and then finished his thought. "Angry sons make insensitive husbands, and they become bad fathers." I listened quietly to his point. "If you're looking for baggage that you're bringing into your marriage, that's where I'd look. That anger is like a pinball rolling around inside of you. And eventually it's going to land somewhere. Unless you unpack that baggage first."

Fr. Jim must have been right, because as we talked about what happened between my dad and me, I felt myself getting angry. There was one image in particular that kept coming back to my mind. When my dad called me into his office that day to fire me, he never closed his office door. He purposely kept it open. He wanted to make sure that everyone in the office heard him as he lambasted and then fired me. Why? In his mind, his law firm's image was at stake. He wanted the word to get out right away in the legal community that Harry Alexopoulos' law firm didn't accept losing, and Harry would go so far as to fire his own son to prove it.

I remember standing in front of my dad that day. The message from him was loud and clear: his law firm's image meant more to him than his relationship with me.

Did that fill me with anger? Probably. But it's one thing to know you are angry, and it's another thing to know how to get rid of all that anger. How do you do that?

Chapter Thirty

It took me several weeks, but I finally had divided up all of our family photographs and videos and delivered one set to my mom's house and another set to the guard gate at the new apartment complex where my Dad was living. That night, my dad picked them up at the gate and took them back to his apartment.

As he walked into his apartment, he put his takeout food on the kitchen counter and placed the boxes of photographs and videos on his kitchen table. He didn't touch his dinner, but instead quickly opened the boxes and began to sift through them, eager to revisit those memories.

How strange it was that all these memories that he'd given up meant so much to him suddenly.

As he sifted through our old family albums, he looked at photos we'd taken through the years: backyard barbeques, birthday parties, graduations, Christmas, holidays. He studied the pictures intently. He'd put one down and then quickly go to another. They say a picture is worth a thousand words, but only three words rang out of these pictures: he wasn't there.

In so many of these pictures, he was simply absent.

He opened another box, hoping that he would be present in these family memories. He sorted through my childhood photos, but in picture after picture all he'd see was my mom, Angie, and me. He flipped through some old report cards from grade school and pulled out a piece of paper that was wedged in one. It was a stick drawing that I made for him many years ago, a crayon picture I'd drawn of Dad and me tossing a football. I'd drawn him in his work clothes and showed us playing on our front lawn. On the bottom of the picture, I'd written, "Dad, will you play with me?"

Sadness came over my dad as he looked at the drawing. I doubt he'd ever seen it before. He put the drawing on the table and continued to stare at it wondering what was so important in his life that he had missed all of this.

He went back to the box and pulled out more photos of Angie and me. He seemed to be studying each one of them as though he didn't know the people in the pictures. Finally, almost as though defeated, he put them back in the boxes and closed them. He took off his reading glasses and reclined in his chair. Alone in an empty apartment: this is where success had taken him.

Bells chimed as my dad entered the church on a quiet winter day. He had brought paperwork to complete the divorce so he could receive dispensation from the church in order to be permitted to still receive Holy Communion. Fr. Jim greeted him and asked him to have a seat in his office. As my dad sat with the paperwork on his lap, he spoke quietly to Fr. Jim. The divorce and all that transpired around it had taken a toll on him, and talking to Fr. Jim was cathartic.

"Do you think you were a good father to Michael?" asked Fr. Jim.

"No. And I have to live with that."

"What do you think you did wrong?"

"When I first started my practice, we were so broke that I had to run my law practice out of my house. And every time I had to meet a client, I'd have to sneak out of the house so Michael wouldn't see me leaving. Angie was fine, but Michael, he'd cry and scream for me to hold him. I'd go down the back steps, out the window, through the garage … anything … all that mattered was that I was on time to see the client."

He looked out the window at the trees that were bare from winter storms. "Now, I look back, and I keep trying to remember Michael as a kid … and I can't remember him. Even when I look at photographs or videos, I don't really remember him. But the clients—I remember every detail about them: case history, rulings, all the appeals … everything. Just like it was yesterday." He looked down and shook his head slightly. "I wish I could go back, but ..."

"What about now? Can't you make up for lost time?

"Did he tell you I fired him a few years ago?"

Fr. Jim nodded his head and then spoke up. "Why do you think you fired him? I mean, big wins, big losses, that comes with the territory in your work, doesn't it?"

"Not in my firm." He leaned in towards Fr. Jim. "Father, my dad came to this country and couldn't speak or read a lick of English. He cleaned tables and washed dishes, finally saved up enough money and got himself a little bar. Still worked seven days a week. But it was his place, and he was proud of it. He ended up losing the bar because of a legal technicality in his contract. He had to go back to washing dishes in the same darn building. Do you know what it's like to watch your father, in his seventies, washing dishes just to make ends meet? But he never complained. The only thing he ever said to me was, 'Get a 'ducation.' He couldn't even pronounce the word. But that's what I did … I got my 'ducation."

As my dad spoke, the frustration of what happened to his father made his voice rise. "They pay me five hundred fifty dollars an hour to do what I do. And you know where I bank every check I get? The bank right next to the cemetery where they buried my old man. Because every time I go to deposit my check, I pass by there, and I hold up that check and I say, 'Dad, I got them back for you. I got my 'ducation."

He looked back out the window. "I wasn't going to let my firm fail. Anything that got in the way of it had to go."

"Even if it was your son?"

"Even if it was my son." He exhaled, having let it all out. "Like I said, now I have to live with that."

Fr. Jim was smart. He said very little. My dad was used to arguing. But that didn't happen that day. Instead, the only words that echoed in that room were his own. The reasoning he heard was his alone, and he would have to process what he had done on his own. A long pause passed between them.

My Dad then got up and handed the piece of paper he'd been holding to Fr. Jim.

"Anyway, here's the statement you needed," said my dad.

"There are a few more steps after this. I'll be in touch."

I had seen my Dad in some big lawsuits. I had seen him under tremendous pressure, but I don't think I'd ever seen him look so exhausted. He was carrying a burden that slowed him down immeasurably as he headed out of Fr. Jim's office.

Chapter Thirty-one

Seeing your client get picked apart on the witness stand by the apposing attorney is always difficult. Your brain is constantly in damage-control mode. You know the exact answer you want your client to give, and they never get close to it. They will look you in the eye five minutes before they take the stand and tell you exactly what they are going to say. Then they get up on the witness stand and say something completely different. As I watched Mr. Witherspoon up on the stand, being taken apart by Surhoff, who was slicing him up like a skilled surgeon, I was grateful that at least my client wasn't deviating from his story and making things worse for himself.

"So, for eight years you never made child support payments for your son?" barked Surhoff.

"Well, I had some debt that …"

"Non-responsive. Move to strike, your honor."

"Yes or no, Mr. Witherspoon," said the judge.

"Did you make any payments, Mr. Witherspoon?"

"Well, no."

"And you say you visited your son, but you have no record of that."

"Correct."

"Ever been to a teacher-parent day at his school?"

"No."

"Ever been to his swimming lessons, help him with his homework, or take care of him when he was sick?"

"No."

I knew Mr. Witherspoon's answers didn't sound good, but at least he was answering directly and honestly. When the witness keeps trying to justify their actions and duck questions, the jury can turn against them.

Before Mr. Witherspoon had taken the stand, I promised him I would rehabilitate him on cross-examination.

"How many phone conversations have you had with your son in the last year?" asked Surhoff.

"Probably about … six."

"And you are requesting fifty percent custody of your son, correct?"

"Yes."

"No further questions." As the Judge motioned to me, I felt it went just about as badly as I thought it would. Now I wanted to see how much I could clean it up.

"Mr. Witherspoon, why weren't you at your son's swimming lessons? Why didn't you help him with his homework?" I asked as I approached him at the witness stand.

"Maxine wouldn't let me see him. I didn't know what to do?"

"Why weren't you paying child support?"

"I had a lot of credit card debt. I was out of work. I paid her whatever I could."

"Have you paid off your credit card debt?"

"Yes. All of it."

"And you have a job, now?"

"Yes. I'm a bus driver for the city."

"Mr. Surhoff mentioned that you rarely called your son. Why was that?"

"She kept changing her phone number. The only time I could speak to my son was when she called me."

"Nothing further."

Short and sweet, to the point: not bad, I thought. Some damage, but we were about to call his son to the stand, and I knew this would override whatever damage just happened. We were still in striking distance of our goal. The judge asked Surhoff if he had any further questions, and he said he didn't. As I walked back to our table, I asked Todd for an honest appraisal of the jury. I knew Todd wouldn't pull any punches with me.

"They're on the fence. The son has got to be strong for us," said Todd.

Once in awhile I wish Todd would lie to me. I was hoping for, "We've got them right where we want them," or "They didn't lay a glove on you." Just a little wind at my back before we got to our key witness. But, that's why Todd and I were friends. He told it like it was, and I knew he was right.

"Mr. Alexopoulos, call you next witness," the judge barked.

"Your honor we'd like to call Thomas Witherspoon at this time," I said. Out of the corner of my eye, I saw Surhoff shoot up out of his chair.

"Your honor, we'd like to request a sidebar at this time," said Surhoff. No way, I thought. Absolutely no way was he going to mess with this witness. This witness was my only shot at winning this case. The judge motioned us to the side of his bench.

"Your honor, in the court's psychologist's recommendation, he stated that the ultimate decision for whether the child should appear in court was yours and we—" said Surhoff.

I cut him off before he could say another word. I was not going to let him bully me or the judge. "He stated that he thought the child was stable enough to appear before the court and—" I barked back.

"May I finish?"

"Alright, knock it off, you two," said the judge.

"I have a sworn deposition by his school teachers that Tommy has been sick for two weeks and has been missing school because he's so worried about appearing here today," Surhoff continued.

"He's sick because he's afraid he might not ever get to see his father again. That's the reason the psychologist wanted him to testify!"

"Alright, enough, enough," said the judge. I couldn't believe we were having this conversation, and that the judge was listening to Surhoff's nonsense.

"Mr. Alexopoulos, I tend to agree with Mr. Surhoff. I hate having kids testify. They're confused. It's traumatic. You've made your case, let—" said Judge Hinderland.

"Your honor, that kid is my case. You take him away, and I'm stuck with twelve female jurors."

"Whose fault is that Mr. Alexopoulos?" said the judge as he stared over the top of his reading glasses at me. "I'm not allowing the child to testify," he said. And with that, he motioned Surhoff and I back to our seats. There are grey areas of law where a judge can put his fingerprint on a case. If they like the way you are handling your case, they lean your way in those areas. If they don't, they lean the other way. Judge Hinderland had just sent me a message, he didn't care for my selecting an all-female jury, and he was sticking it to me. I also found out later that my dad had been before him several times, and they had argued extensively with each other in those cases. Judges have memories like elephants, and this was a little payback.

"Mr. Alexopoulos, call your next witness."

"No further witnesses your honor. We'll rest at this time."

"Alright, let's call it a day. We'll pick it up tomorrow morning with closing arguments." I picked up my briefcase and glanced over at Surhoff who was all smiles as he exited the courtroom. He and I both knew that for all intents and purposes, I had just lost this case.

Chapter Thirty-two

I was a half hour late to see Sophia for dinner. As I entered Delphino's Restaurant, I saw Sophia seated off to the side. I made my way over to her table. I didn't want to burden her with how awful my day had been.

"Sorry, I'm late. Long day in court," I said. As I got my menu from the waiter, I could see something was wrong with Sophia as she was unusually quiet.

"Everything okay with you?"

"Not really."

"What's the matter?"

"I met with Fr. Jim today. We were going over the wedding ceremony. And he told me there are no vows in the ceremony. You just go around a table three times together and that's it. You're husband and wife."

I took a deep breath. After what just happened in court, I needed to shift gears and deal with this. I explained to Sophia that we don't just walk around a table three times. The service is over an hour long and is very detailed.

"But, there are no vows," she said.

"When you go around the table that symbolizes your first steps together. It's like saying your vows."

"But, I wanted to hear those words, Michael."

"Which words?"

"All the days of my life. I just want to know that that's the promise we're making to each other: that we'll be together forever." I was worn out and didn't have the energy to go into a long, detailed response.

"Sophia, they are not going to change the service just for us."

"You don't seem upset by it."

"Because I know how I feel about you. I don't need to hear those words."

"You don't need to hear those words? Well, I guess we have different perceptions about what's happening on our wedding day."

Sophia got up and left the restaurant. I leaned back in my chair, exhausted. This wasn't my day.

I drove back to Sophia's apartment and got there a few minutes after she had arrived. Sophia was sitting at her kitchen table with a box of tissues, crying, when I rang her doorbell. "C'mon, get your coat on," I said. She grabbed her coat, and we walked out to my car. A light snow began to fall as we drove along in silence. After a few minutes, Sophia spoke up.

"Where are we going?"

"Close your eyes," I told her. She closed her eyes, as I continued down the road. At a cul-de-sac, I brought the car to a stop. I flipped my high beams on. I got out of the car and came around to her side and opened the door.

"Open your eyes," I said. She opened them and saw that my high beams had illuminated a bank of snow. She looked at it puzzled. I proceeded over to the snow drift and dug through the snow with my hands, pulling back shrubbery and soot, until I found what I was looking for: the battered carving in the tree house. I pulled the piece she'd carved it on free, and I held it up so the high beams would illuminate it for her to read. As the light bounced off it, Sophia saw the sign clearly.

"Sophia and Michael ... forever"

I came back over to the car and turned on the CD player to play, "Rocky Top." Sophia got out of the car, and we walked out into the stream of light that shot out from the high beams. I took her arms and we began to dance slowly in front of the sign, just as we had so many years before. After a few moments, I looked at Sophia.

"I'm not going anywhere, Sophia," I said. "And if it takes the rest of my life to prove that to you, I will."

All the angst that was pent up inside of her slowly melted away as she relaxed into my arms. As the night air whipped around us, I looked at her face. It was as peaceful as

I'd remembered it back when we were just kids.

The fireplace in my apartment crackled, and I looked over and saw Sophia sleeping in front of it. I was sitting at the kitchen table writing on a legal pad, trying to come up with my closing arguments for our custody case. The balled up wads of paper that were around me were a testament to my many un-successful attempts so far. A moment later, Sophia woke up and looked over.

"Any luck?" she said.

"No."

"Go back, Michael. Why did you take this case in the first place?"

"Money," I said. "We needed the money." Just then, the doorbell rang. I opened the door and saw my dad standing there holding some food and a hanger with a bag over it.

"I figured you'd be up late tonight. Thought you'd need a little food," my dad said. He handed me a pizza box and some soda. I thanked him, and then there was an awkward pause. "If you need any help,

Falling in Love with Sophia

I could help you organize some of your
points," my dad offered.

"Thanks, Dad. But, I've got to figure this
one out by myself."

"The jury is still listening, Michael."

"I overplayed the kid."

"Don't worry about the kid. It's you and
Surhoff, now." I nodded at my father's assur-
ance. Then he handed me the hanger with a
bag over it to me.

"I got you a little something …" I un-
zipped the bag and saw he had bought me a
beautiful new suit. "It's a little thing, but ju-
ries appreciate it … it tells them that you believe they're important." There was another
awkward beat, before my dad spoke up.

"You know Michael, for whatever it's
worth, I've got sixty-five lawyers who work
with me, some of the best in this city, but if
I ever got in trouble, I'd have you represent
me. Not because you're my son, but because
I think you're that good a lawyer."

With that, my dad headed down the
steps, got into his car, and left. I walked back
into the apartment and sat quietly next to
Sophia.

"Was that your dad?" she asked.

I nodded.

"You know what's always frustrated me, Michael? I look at you and your dad, and I think how lucky you are that you still have each other. I wish I had that, and it's frustrating to see both of you let all this time go by and not work things out."

She was right. My dad and I should have worked through our problems. But, like a garden hose that gets so twisted up, how in the world could we begin to untangle them? It's not easy. I thought back to the genealogy map that Sophia had at work.

"You know when you were talking about settling accounts and making peace with your past? How do you do that?" I asked her.

"Everybody does it their own way." She leaned in and did what only Sophia could do. She cut to the heart of the matter and set my sails in the right direction. "Michael, you didn't take this case for the money. You took it because you knew this was the last chance that Mr. Witherspoon had to connect with his son. And if you lost, at least there would be a public record so the son could know how badly his dad wanted to be with him."

She sat down next to me. "How do broken relationships settle their accounts?" Sophia asked me. She took my pen and legal pad and put it in front of me. "I think you know the answer. Now, just tell the jury," she said.

Chapter Thirty-three

The stunning view from my Dad's office had never looked better. A storm had cleared the air, and you could see up and down the lakefront. A group of lawyers from his firm were gathered around a large circular table wrapping up their weekly meeting. The lawyers were going over all their cases, as my Dad peacefully stared out the window, taking in the view.

"Anybody else have any other business?" asked an attorney." He looked over to my Dad, "Harry, what about you?"

My dad gazed out the window for a lingering moment. "Amazing view isn't it?" he mused, as though he'd never fully noticed it before. A few nodded as others prepared for the meeting to come to an end after my father spoke. He looked back at the group of lawyers, and then turned his chair around slightly. "I'm going to start laying off my case load to all of you," my dad said flatly. There was a bit of an awkward pause.

"Are you going on vacation?" asked one of the attorneys.

"No."

"Do you have a health issue or something?"

"No." he said flatly. "I'm just cutting back. And it may be permanent." It suddenly got very quiet in the room. My dad got up and headed for the door. All the lawyers looked around nervously, and then one of them spoke up.

"Uh, Harry … is there anything more you need to tell us?" My father stopped, looked at the group and then spoke.

"I had a client come in recently. He'd been in a car accident. Car flipped upside down, and he was trapped underneath it. He was bleeding badly, and he thought he was dying. As he was lying there, he noticed a pen had landed near him. He was able to grab it with his fingertips. And on the car seat, he was barely able to scribble a few words, which he thought were going to be the last words of his life.

"You know what he wrote?" The group was silent, listening to my father.

"I love my wife. I love my children." My dad looked from one end of the room to the other. "I love my wife. I love my children." He stared at the carpet and paused before continuing.

"The guy was thirty-five years old, had a broken pelvis, collapsed lung, and ended up in the hospital for two months. But he survived. As I sat across from him, I kept thinking, he was the luckiest guy in the world, not just because he survived, but because for the rest of his life, he'd always have his priorities straight."

The room was absolutely silent as my dad finished his thoughts.

"I love my wife. I love my children."

And with that Harry Alexopoulos turned and quietly exited the room. I'm not sure if my father fully knew the change that was occurring in his life, but after that day, he would never practice law again.

Chapter Thirty-four

On the days when I was trying a case in court, everything seemed amplified. I'm sure it was business as usual for everyone else, but to me, everything seemed so much louder, so much more intense. And the day we had to give closing arguments on the Witherspoon case was no different. As I walked through the courthouse, the energy seemed so heightened and the distractions were plentiful.

Unfortunately, there seems to be only one place where I can collect my thoughts without someone interrupting: a stall in the bathroom. So, that's where I went. In the bathroom, no one bothers you so you can collect your thoughts, and if your nerves get the best of you and you have to throw up, you are at the right place.

Down the hall, the elevator doors opened and Surhoff came running around the corner to get in. Sophia, Angie, *Yia Yia* Penelope and Jerome were already in the elevator. Surhoff looked over at them.

"Morning," he said. Sophia, Angie and Jerome nodded back at Surhoff but not *Yia Yia*. She wasn't going to exchange phony pleasantries with Surhoff. She gave him the best cold shoulder she could give. Then, not being able to restrain herself, she said to Jerome in Greek, "He's the devil."

Jerome nodded and said in Greek, "I know."

Surhoff slowly turned and looked at the two of them, wondering what was just said. They kept looking straight ahead. He went back to adjusting some files in his legal briefcase. *Yia Yia*, Sophia, Angie and Jerome quietly looked over at him and in unison shot him a Greek wave. Surhoff, feeling a bit uneasy, turned to look at them, but they just stared ahead, looking innocent. A moment later, they all got off the elevator, heading in different directions. Sophia turned to *Yia Yia* and said, "What does that mean, again?"

"Ah, just a little curse."

They headed into the courtroom, and a moment later, I entered. The judge called everyone to order, and just as we were about to proceed, the back doors of the court-room opened and two-dozen lawyers from Surhoff's law firm entered. All eyes in the courtroom, most notably the jurors, were on them. This is just what Surhoff wanted.

These attorneys were there for two rea-sons: one, they thought Surhoff walked on water and they wanted to see the maestro at work, and two, they wanted to intimidate both me and the jury. They were trying to tell the jury that this attorney must be great, if so many of his peers came to watch him.

Surhoff began his closing arguments, and he left no stone unturned. He moved around the courtroom pounding away at my client. What struck me was how hard he was trying. He wasn't phoning this in. Maybe it was my tirade in his office that made him want this so bad. Maybe it was the impor-tance of this client that made him want to win now that he had taken the case to trial. Whatever it was, he was giving it his all.

"He wasn't there for any parent-child conferences!" he bellowed. "He wasn't there for the doctor's visits, the homework, the swimming lessons, the comforting in the middle of the night. And, yet, now, we are supposed to believe that suddenly he will do all those things we know a good father should do." As Surhoff continued, I noticed my dad quietly enter the courtroom.

"You don't have to wonder if he can do it. You don't have to guess if he can do it. Just look at his track record. It tells you who he is: a man who is in no way ready or deserving of this kind of responsibility." Surhoff finished and sauntered over to his table. He had delivered the goods, and he knew it.

"Mr. Alexopoulos, you're next," said the judge. I sat in my chair for a moment, looking towards the jury. A peace came over me. I knew I had a story to tell.

"Fathers and sons," I said. I still hadn't moved from my chair. "What a complex and emotional subject." My eyes looked at each of the jurors. "Does your father love you?" I got up and began walking slowly towards the jurors. "Do you love your father? Do you hate your father? Did the two of you get to express how you felt towards each other or did time run out on you. And now one of you is left hoping for a better day when all the crooked lines will become straight and all these matters that contort our emotions will be laid to rest. When we will be able to fully express our thoughts, our disappointments, our mistakes … our love to each other."

I gestured to Mr. Witherspoon. "Today is that better day for Mr. Witherspoon. You decide whether he gets to have that conversation with his son." I walked back in front of the jurors. Out of the corner of my eye, I could see my dad intently watching from his seat. "I want you to think about your father for a moment. What's your best memory of him? Was it a fancy dinner he took you to? Probably not."

I walked over to the other end of the juror booth speaking directly to each juror. "Was it an expensive present he bought you for Christmas or your birthday? Probably not. You know what I think we remember most about our fathers?" I paused and looked at all of the jurors.

"The time they spent with us."

I moved closer to the jurors. "Because when they give us their time, they give us their smile, they give us their hug, they give us their laughter … they give us their love. What a gift."

The jurors were locked in as my eyes moved from one to the next. "That's what we're fighting for here, today: time. Time for this father to spend with his son."

I looked back towards Mr. Witherspoon who was listening as closely as the jurors were to what I had to say.

"Now, maybe some of you didn't like your father. Maybe some of you didn't even know your father. If that's the case, then you're the ones I need to go back into the jury room and tell the others how much it would have meant to you to have a father who loved you, to have a father who cared about you, to have a father who wanted to spend time with you." As I turned, I could see Sophia watching over me, pulling for me every step of the way.

"Has Mr. Witherspoon made mistakes? Sure he has. And he's worked very hard to correct those mistakes. But how do we come to terms with the fact that he's made mistakes? How do we settle that account? You know, it's a funny thing that all of us sons go through. As we get older in life, we don't see our dads so much as a father anymore, but we start to see him as a man. And we start to see all his shortcomings, his foibles, his humanity, and his mistakes.

"And right when we are about to cast judgment on him, something wonderful happens. We get married and start having children of our own. And we start making mistakes of our own. And we can't help but realize that someday we are going to be judged by our children for the mistakes we've made. And our children will make a decision to condemn us or forgive us for the mistakes we've made. That's the decision you have to make today. Do you condemn the father for his mistakes or do you forgive the father?" I stood back from the jurors and delivered my final thought.

"I say the answer is forgiveness."

The courtroom was silent. As I turned and headed back to my seat, I saw my father with his head bowed, wiping tears from his eyes. I had only seen my dad cry twice in my life. Once, on the day his mother was buried and the other, that day in court.

Chapter Thirty-five

After the judge gave the jury some final instructions, he dismissed them. There was no decision that day. I wasn't sure how to read that. There was a moment right after I finished my closing arguments that I thought I had done well. That feeling lasted for about three minutes, and then I started worrying about everything I had done in the case. By the next morning, I was resolved that we had probably lost. As we sat in a diner near the courthouse, Sophia, Mr. Witherspoon, and Todd kept me company. Stan and Angie were off in another corner, actually holding hands as they talked. As happy as I was to see that, I couldn't help but look at my watch and wonder what was holding the jury up.

At another table, *Yia Yia* Penelope sat with all the other *yia yias*. She looked over at me. "He's nervous," she said. She turned to them with a look of last resort on her face. "What do you think?" *Yia Yia* Penelope asked.

She looked at the *yia yias* and got a series of nods. "Okay. Let's do it, then," she said.

With gusto, all the *yia yias* turned over their Greek coffee cups onto the saucers underneath them and then flipped the cups back upright again. As the remaining contents dripped down the inside of the cup, the *yia yias* began their expert reading of the cup. Some Greeks believe with absolute certainty that they can tell your future by reading the drippings off the inside of a coffee cup. Depending on how the remnants formed along the inside edges of the cup, they swore they could tell your future.

"Good news," said one *yia yia* with certainty, as she pointed to a high ridge of coffee remnants in her cup.

"Yep. I see good news, too," said another.

"Oh, yeah. Big success," said *Yia Yia* Penelope pointing at her cup. As the *yia yias* analyzed their cups further, the diner door opened and my dad walked in. "Michael, the jury's back," he said. Everyone got up in a hurry and began to exit. As they did, Stan leaned over to one of the *yia yias*.

"You can't get stock tips off those cups, can you?" asked Stan.

"We'll talk," said one of the *yia yias* with confidence.

The courtroom was buzzing as the jurors entered. Mr. Witherspoon, Todd, and I watched nervously from our table on one side of the room, while Surhoff, his staff, and Maxine watched from the other side of the room. All of the attorneys from Surhoff's office were there, no doubt to celebrate with him.

"Madame Forewoman, I understand you've reached a verdict on this matter," said the judge.

"Yes, we have your honor."

"Please hand it to the court clerk." The forewoman handed the verdict to the clerk. The court clerk read it loud, and her voice echoed off the walls.

"We the jury, in the above titled matter as it relates to the custody of Thomas

Witherspoon find in favor of the Plaintiff, Peter Witherspoon. And that his request for equal and joint custody of his son Thomas Witherspoon shall hereby be granted to him."

We won. I heard the words, but I didn't really react. I had been losing for so long that I forgot what winning felt like. Mr. Witherspoon was overcome with joy. He hugged me before I could even get my hands up to hug him back.

I was trying to keep my professional decorum, but I couldn't suppress a smile that broke out over my face. This victory had been a long time coming.

I turned to Todd and we congratulated each other. I then turned and looked for Sophia. Through her tears, she smiled back at me. I looked back and saw *Yia Yia*. She just nodded at me and smiled as her right hand tugged on the cross she wore around her neck.

Before I headed out of the courtroom, I glanced over at Surhoff. He was stunned, dazed, and confused. If I had forgotten what winning felt like, it was clear that he'd forgotten what losing felt like. All the attorneys around him looked lost. They didn't seem to know what to do or what to say to him. I didn't realize it at that moment, but I had made a name for myself that day. I had slain the proverbial dragon. When I looked back years later, I realized that our law practice grew substantially from that day forth because of what happened.

The courtroom emptied out into the hallway. It seemed like everyone who'd ever met me at the courthouse was coming up to congratulate me. They were happy because, more than anything else, they couldn't stand Surhoff and were glad to see him get beaten. Then I saw my father. I excused myself and made my way over to him. I had never seen my dad so happy.

"Congratulations, counselor," he said proudly. He gestured to all my friends nearby. "I know you've got things to do. I won't take up your time."

"No, don't worry about it, Dad," I said.

"Boy, that was something," he said, still beaming. He looked around at the beauty and grandeur of the courthouse. A softness came over him. It was almost like watching a great athlete taking one last look across the field he had played on. "I've had a lot of great days here. But I'll tell you, I've never had a day like you had in there today." He gestured towards the courtroom. "God almighty, that was beautiful, Michael." His eyes turned back towards me. "Anyway, I just wanted you to know how, um …" He shook his head slightly, unable to find the right words. I knew what he was trying to say.

"I understand, Dad. You don't—"

He smiled and laughed at himself. "Harry Alexopoulos at a loss for words. That's funny. Well, this is good for the old man." He gathered his thoughts and looked down towards the floor. "I know I've missed the mark a few times along the way, and I regret that. I can't tell you how much I wish I had some of those hours back. Anyway, I'm going to be taking some time off from work."

"To do what?" I asked.

"Nothing."

I smiled and nodded. After seeing my dad work so hard his whole life, it would be fun to see him do nothing for awhile.

"I thought once you and Sophia come home from your honeymoon and get settled in, it'd be great to see you and … spend some time together. Talk about things."

"I'd like that."

Just then, someone from the courtroom crowd yelled out to me. I motioned that I'd be right over.

"Hey, they're waiting for the champ. I won't keep you any longer." My dad pulled out an envelope, handed it to me. "This will cover the rest of the expenses for the wedding."

"No, c'mon Dad …"

"Hey, we had a verbal agreement, counselor." He stuffed the check in my pocket. "I did take a little deduction out of there as my referral fee for this case." I paused for a moment and looked at the smile on his face.

"You're the one who referred Mr. Witherspoon to me?" His smile said it all. My dad had referred Mr. Witherspoon to me, and that is how this whole thing got started. I looked over to Mr. Witherspoon who smiled. My dad put his arms on my shoulders and spoke to me as only a father could. "Listen,

Michael Harry Alexopoulos, you take Sophia and you wrap your arms around each other and shoot straight for the moon. All the stars, the constellations, that beautiful sea of lights are waiting for you. And it's a wonderful journey, kiddo. Don't ever let anyone tell you it's not." He paused and then finished his thoughts. "I'm proud of you."

He gave me a hug and quickly made his way to the exit as I made my way back over to Sophia and our friends.

We had won. Victory felt great. I couldn't wait to celebrate.

What I learned at Church Camp – Lesson #7

"Celebrate with a little humility."

Every night the counselors planned some activities to keep us busy. It could be anything from a singing contest to an air guitar contest. On this particular night, they decided to have a bubble gum blowing contest: whichever counselor or camper blew the biggest bubble won.

They created complex brackets, eliminations, semi-finals, final eight, and then the championship rounds. Now, chewing bubble gum was not big in my family. My mother thought we looked like cows when we chewed it, so my experience with bubble gum was definitely limited. However, for some reason I found myself doing pretty well and winning in the early rounds. As each passing round went by, I defeated every participant. Who needed softball I thought?

Finally, it came down to three participants: me, Teddy K., and a counselor. We all started blowing our final bubble. I couldn't believe it. Mine just kept getting bigger and bigger. Moments later, I heard the other two contestants' bubbles pop. That was it. I was the undisputed Bubble Gum Blowing Champion of the Church Camp. You might think that I took my bow, got off the stage, and decided to celebrate with a little humility. But, no. Somehow I decided that it was a perfect moment to speak about how Jesus had guided me to victory in becoming the undisputed Bubble Gum Blowing Champion. I wish I was making this up, but I'm not. I started out by saying, "This is a perfect example of how Jesus works in our lives." Oh, brother. After that, everything that came out of my mouth was one step short of a Bubble Gum Sermon on the Mount. "Blessed are the Bubble Gum blowers for they shall inherit the earth," and so on. I'm surprised that I didn't take one piece of bubble gum and try and multiply it into many pieces so everyone could partake.

Years later, I thought that maybe I had over exaggerated in my mind what an idiot I made of myself that day. That was until I ran into Teddy K., and he confirmed that I had in fact delivered a sermon. The good news was that Teddy had gone on to be a state senator, and as far as I could tell, he seemed to have recovered from the devastating loss.

Lesson learned: God loves humility.

Chapter Thirty-six

After our great victory, we made our way back outside of our law offices. Todd and I said goodbye to Mr. Witherspoon who was grabbing a coffee at Carlos' Cart. As always, Carlos had the music cranked up. Mr. Witherspoon sipped his coffee as he walked over to a cab we'd called for him. "You changed my life. Thank you both for everything," he said.

"You're welcome Mr. Witherspoon," we both said. As he was about to get into the cab, I asked him one last question. "Hey, Mr. Witherspoon, you don't happen to have an extra picture of your son, do you?"

Mr. Witherspoon paused and smiled at me. "I thought you didn't let yourself get caught up in that stuff anymore? You know pictures of clients, and stuff like that."

"Did I say that?" I said to him with a smile. "I like pictures. Pictures are good."

Mr. Witherspoon laughed and reached into his suit coat pocket, almost as though he were just waiting for me to ask. "You know, I just happen to have an extra one on me." He handed it to me, and I took a long look at his beautiful son. "He's a beautiful kid. Make sure you bring him around so I can see him grow up."

"I will," said Mr. Witherspoon.

I tucked the picture away, as Mr. Witherspoon smiled and got into the taxi. Todd and I paused for a moment. We looked up and gazed at the O'Malley, Surhoff, and Kraft building. What a great moment this was to stare at the defeated Goliath. Without saying anything to each other, we both started to laugh. Just then, Carlos, who was cleaning his cart up and closing for the day, turned his music up even louder. Todd, hearing the music, started dancing in front of the mammoth offices of O'Malley, Surhoff, and Kraft. It didn't take more than a few seconds before I was joining him. We did everything from the robot to the twist and even threw in a little

Greek dancing. As the music played, the two of us made idiots out of ourselves dancing all around with our briefcases in front of the fountain area, and it felt great.

We danced in front of the ground floor cafeteria of the building and happened to look in and see none other than Surhoff. He was being read the riot act by Maxine. He looked over and saw Todd and me. We paused for a moment. Maybe we were rubbing it in a bit too much, I thought. You know that lesson about winning and humility that I learned at Church camp? Well, I guess I still hadn't quite learned the lesson well enough yet, because we broke into something that looked like an Irish Lord of the Dance routine right in front of the window. We were thrilled, and Surhoff was miserable. Order had been restored in the universe.

Chapter Thirty-seven

The church was decked out for our wedding day. Flowers lined the pews and lay strewn throughout the rest of the church. In one of the waiting rooms, Sophia double-checked her hair and makeup. Her mother and all the *yia yias* were busy helping her with last minute touches. Just then, Fr. Jim knocked and entered. "Okay, everyone, it's time. Let's get started," he said.

"Okay. I'm ready," said Sophia. All the *yia yias* turned and gazed at Sophia. She turned back to Fr. Jim.

"I mean … I'll be ready in a few minutes." She then smiled at him, and said, "Greek time." Fr. Jim shook his head and muttered to himself as he walked out the door. "Off all the traditions to teach her …"

Inside the church, a large crowd of people gathered in the pews as the bridesmaids began walking down the aisle. Angie was escorted by Stan, and all the *yia yias* smiled a knowing smile. They knew theirs would be the next wedding they would be attending. Angie smiled at Todd and gestured as though the imaginary golden handcuffs had been unlocked.

Sophia entered the front of the church, looking radiant in her wedding gown. As her mother smoothed out her dress, Sophia looked over and saw Jerome waiting for her. He was dressed in a tuxedo and was the epitome of a gentleman.

"Look at you," Sophia said to Jerome.

"And look at you," said Jerome. As everyone got into their final places, Sophia took Jerome's arm. She looked up at him.

"You know how much you mean to me, don't you?" said Sophia. Jerome smiled at her and started to get emotional. "Oh, don't you start now ..." said Jerome.

"Through all the bad times, you were my anchor, Jerome. I couldn't have asked for anyone more special to hold my hand on this walk. You're part of my family. I know my dad is smiling down on us today."

Sophia reached up and wiped a tear away from his eye. "The bride is supposed to be crying not me," said Jerome. They laughed at themselves. Then, after a moment, they heard the music cueing them. "They're playing your music, Ms. Sophia."

Her smile said everything. She was ready. He held up her hand, and she promenaded around him. Then they went through the main doors, entering the church.

As the doors opened, I saw Sophia, beautiful, radiant, precious Sophia. What transpired next is hard to describe, but it was so powerful that it has stayed with me ever since. As Sophia began to walk towards me, everything slowed down and the room became silent. I experienced a feeling that was unlike any other. I've had moments of great joy in my life, but I've never felt a moment like that. All my fears were calmed, all my mistakes were forgiven, and all the love I sought surrounded me. In that moment when God brings two people together to become one, I think with one breath He silences the heavens and summons all the orders that surround him: the archangels, the angels, the saints, and all our loved ones who have passed before us. Together, they peer over the cusp of Heaven in awe of this sacred moment. And in that moment, a moment I will remember the rest of my life, I saw my entire future brought before me: my life to come, my best friend, my lover, my companion, the mother of my children, my defender, my soul mate. My wife.

Sophia walked down the final few steps of the isle to me, and then Jerome gave me her hand. Sophia smiled at me and the service began.

When you are in the pews watching a Greek Orthodox wedding it seems to go on for a long time, but when it is your wedding, it seems to fly by.

Fr. Jim spoke and a reader read from the bible, "Wives submit to your husbands, as to the Lord. For the husband is the head of the wife as God is the head of the Church ... Husbands, love your wives." As the reader continued, Sophia surreptitiously stepped on my foot. I looked over at her, wondering why she'd just done that. She just smiled at me.

"What was that for?" I whispered to her.

"That's a Greek superstition," she said gleefully, barely able to contain her smile. I gave her a quizzical look, having never heard of this particular superstition.

"Whoever steps on the other person's foot first after that passage is read is going to be the boss of the family."

"Where did you learn that one?" I asked her. She smiled and looked back towards *Yia Yia* Penelope. I turned to see little, innocent *Yia Yia* sitting in the pew, smiling back at me. She crossed her leg, and I just about passed out when I saw what she had done. *Yia Yia* had gotten a tattoo on her ankle just like the one Sophia had.

Another *yia yia* who was next to her saw it and turned to her. "What did you do?" she asked incredulously.

"Sometimes you just have to look life right in the eye and say ..." said *Yia Yia* as she did a raspberry just like Sophia had. The other *yia yia* nodded. I hoped these *yia yias* with tattoos weren't starting some sort of trend.

A short while later, the moment had arrived. Sophia and I circled the table three times consecrating our marriage. As we went around, an attendant threw petals in our path while another threw them over our heads.

The ceremony ended, and it was official; Sophia and I were married.

Chapter Thirty-eight

At the reception, raucous, wild bluegrass music blared out and everyone danced. Jerome was in the middle of the room with a microphone shouting out instructions. "Bow to your left, swing to your right, do-si-do ... now promenade," Jerome yelled out. He looked over at me and threw me the cowboy hat. I put it on, went to the middle of the circle, and met all the *yia yias*, Angie, Stan, and Todd. We all did some two-stepping. I looked over and saw Sophia. She couldn't believe it. She started whistling and ran over to join us. As the song came to an end, I took my hat and flung it in the air.

A short time later, we all sat down for dinner, and Todd, who was my best man, introduced my mom as the last speaker of the night. My mom, looking regal and elegant, stood up and made her way to the podium. She held a small wrapped gift in her hands.

"As most of you know, Michael and Sophia are spending part of their honeymoon in San Francisco before they go to Greece." She placed the small gift on the podium. "Now, it may seem a bit tacky, but I thought I would show you the gift that I purchased for them for their wedding. She unwrapped the gift, and I saw a cheap, twelve-inch plastic replica of the Golden Gate Bridge. "I hope it doesn't seem like I'm bragging, but this little gem set me back five dollars and ninety five cents." The audience laughed as she proudly held it up to show them.

"You know, many years ago, I traveled across this bridge on my honeymoon, and over the years, I learned a lot about the bridge. I consider myself kind of an expert on it now." I noticed my dad watching proudly as my mom spoke so eloquently. "You see, when you cross the Golden Gate Bridge, you cross into the city of love. And you'll notice something on the bridge: workers. At the beginning of every year, workers start at one end of the bridge to touch it up. Sometimes the bridge needs a little paint, sometimes the bolts need tightening, sometimes the tension on the wires needs to be released."

I looked around the room and saw that everyone was listening intently as she spoke. "Through the wind, the fog, and the rain, the workers make their way across the bridge fixing all the little problems. And at the end of the year, they finally make it to the other side. But a new year has begun, and so they go right back to the beginning and start the whole process all over again. That's how they keep the bridge in perfect condition." She put the replica back on the podium. "Because, they realize that if you keep that bridge in good condition, your passage to the city of love will always be a joyous one." She lifted her glass.

"To Michael and Sophia. May you forever be able to cross over into your city of love."

My dad was the first one to hoist his drink and applaud, and the rest of the room followed. I heard a wave of clanking glasses. I leaned over and exchanged a kiss with Sophia.

A few minutes later, Costas and his band were playing music full out. Everyone started towards the floor. Even my mom and dad joined in the same line to Greek dance together. I overheard him tell her what a great speech she gave, and she thanked him. I turned to Sophia.

"You know, there's an old saying ..." I said it in Greek and then in English, "You've come to the dance, now it's time to dance."

I picked up a crisp white napkin off the table, extended it to Sophia, and she took it. The Greek band played one of the traditional first songs entitled, *"Orea Poune E Nifee Mas"* ("How Beautiful Our Bride Is"). And how beautiful Sophia was. As the music played, Sophia and I glided across the floor. We turned, spun, and whirled around with gusto. Sophia took the lead, and as she danced, I held her hand and was able to see the absolute joy in her face. It was then that I noticed that she was whipping and twirling the white napkin joyfully in the air, just as she had told me she wanted to do some day. She was free, and it was wonderful to see. As we circled the dance floor, I thought about the sheer happiness I felt when I was that eight-year-old boy dancing across my parents' rug. Once again, I had those three simple things in my life: my culture, my family, and God. Life was beautiful.

What I learned at Church Camp

The Final Lesson

Church camp had ended. I returned home and began the school year. It was at the beginning of that year that I met Sophia. I wanted to spend as much time as I could with her so I could get to know her. We were both too young to officially date, so it was tough trying to find time to spend together. One night, she told me about a Bible study she went to and asked if I'd like to go with her. I would have gone to a yodeling contest with her. So, I said sure. I didn't quite anticipate my parents' and *Yia Yia's* reaction. *Yia Yia* immediately started telling everyone I'd joined a cult, and every day for the rest of the week my dad suddenly read the Bible after dinner. I remember the first night he dramatically divided the bible and said, "This is the Old Testament and this is the New Testament." Oh, brother, I thought, I'm just going to an innocent Bible study. Why is everyone so freaked out?

So, Sophia and I went to the Bible study. We sat in a circle of metal chairs with a large group of other kids and young adults. Sophia knew some of them, but I didn't know any of them. We went around the circle and everyone introduced ourselves, said a little about who we were and what was going on with our lives.

It seemed like everyone was into sports because I recall everyone talking about athletics and how they prayed before games so that God gave them strength. I thought that was pretty cool because I was just starting to get into sports. I could relate to what they were saying.

Then, a young man got up to speak. He had a cast on, and it looked liked he'd broken his arm. I can't remember his name, but he began to speak about what he'd done that past summer. I anticipated him talking about getting hurt in a football game or something like that. However, he told a very different story. He said that he had been working at a church camp over the summer, and one day he'd reached into a large dryer bin and it had torn off his arm from the elbow down. People in the room seemed to fade as my eyes slowly focused on this young man. Could he be the man from my camp?

He talked about how the trip to the hospital had been long, and by the time he got there, the doctors told him they couldn't reattach his arm because too much time had gone by. But when the arm arrived, someone had placed it in salt water and had preserved it. A doctor noticed this and stayed there throughout the night diligently working on reattaching his arm. Eventually this doctor was successful.

I stared at the young man and realized in the traumatic moments of that day at the camp, I never actually saw him or met him. Yet, there he was. It was him.

At the next break, I couldn't help myself. I got up and walked over, looked at him, and then stared at his arm. How could this possibly be? We'd all given up hope. Fr. Angelo had told us that sometimes the answer we get back from God is no. Yet, there this young man's arm was: reattached. I told him I was there that day he lost his arm. I never said anything to him about the salt. That was God's miracle, not mine. As we talked, I couldn't take my eyes off his arm. As I stared at it, he slowly, almost imperceptibly, wiggled his fingers for me. He talked about how the accident had changed his life; for the first time he had a relationship with God. We spoke throughout the Bible study. As the class ended, I said goodbye to him and wished him well.

I never saw him again, and I never went to that Bible study again. It just happened that on that one night when he was there, I happened to be there to witness one of God's miracles. As I walked outside into the fresh autumn air, I talked to Sophia about the young man and the miracle I'd witnessed. A few moments later, my mother picked us up and drove us home. Sophia and I sat in the back seat, innocently holding hands as we looked out the window at the first signs of fall.

Neither of us had any idea that God had already put into motion the plans that He had for our lives.

As I think back to that car ride and all that was to follow, I've come to believe that the lessons I learned at the church camp that summer were true: *God does know the dreams in our hearts* and *He is listening*. There is absolutely no question in my mind that He heard Fay praying on that dusty road so many years ago. Prayers that we've long ago forgotten, God remembers. He heard me say that I wanted to become a lawyer so that I could help people. I had gotten off track working for my dad; I wasn't going to help anyone if I continued working there. I would have helped corporations make more money. But that is not what was in my heart, and God knew it. Sometimes I think God knows us better than we know ourselves.

My dad firing me was necessary to get both me and my father back on track. It was painful to go through, loss of any kind is difficult to take, no question about it. But, I believe that *even at our lowest moments, God is still working*. When we are crying, He is still working. When we are in so much pain that it is hard to look up, He is still working. When we are mad at Him, He is still working. When we are sleeping, He is still working. And through each turn in our lives, through each victory, through each defeat, through each minor decision and major decision, *God is fine tuning us for the victory prepared up ahead.* With *humility*, I've come to know that *God is sacred.* No other person, not a mother, not a father, not a grandparent, will love us, cherish us, and sustain us through our entire life the way God does. Unfortunately, parents, grandparents, and loved ones pass away and can no longer love and protect us, but God's love and protection endures. *Only God, who is a God of order, could plan out the complex details and order of our lives.* He's not only attentive to the minute-to-minute details of our lives, but He also reaches across years, decades, and generations to prepare and map out our individual and collective journeys to perfection. We live in the moment. God lives in eternity. He leaves no detail unattended, and there are no accidents. In fact, as strange as it may sound, I have a feeling that God might have had a purpose in your reading this book. Maybe there is something that He wants to share with you: a thought, a prayer, a hope. How wonderful that would be. Someday, if our paths should cross, it would be great to talk with you about that. It might just be me that needs to be lifted up at that moment, you never know. And maybe I could tell you what happened to Sophia and me. I'm not sure you'd believe it, though. Well, for now, I can tell you this much: it involved three miracles.

Final lesson learned: God is victorious.

To Order a copy of this book:

Call Toll Free at 800-410-8388
or visit us online at:
www.ellinasmultimedia.com